Alfred Austin

Savonarola

A Tragedy

Alfred Austin

Savonarola
A Tragedy

ISBN/EAN: 9783337311445

Printed in Europe, USA, Canada, Australia, Japan

Cover: Foto ©Andreas Hilbeck / pixelio.de

More available books at **www.hansebooks.com**

SAVONAROLA

A TRAGEDY

BY

ALFRED AUSTIN

𝔏𝔬𝔫𝔡𝔬𝔫

MACMILLAN AND CO.

AND NEW YORK

1891

First Edition 1881

Second Edition 1891

DEDICATION

In an epoch distinguished beyond all its predecessors for the plastic activity of our race, the artistic presentation of the Drama has exhibited, as might have been expected, an unprecedented development; and of this refined and elevating movement you have been the most strenuous agent and the most conspicuous figure. Combining with a generous temper and the lavish hand severe judgment and consummate taste, you have embellished and interpreted, with supreme success, the noblest plays in the language.

DEDICATION

It is to your unrivalled achievements in this important province of our national life that I would fain pay my poor tribute of grateful admiration. But I should be expressing only half my thought, did I not at the same time tender to the warm-hearted friend and the intellectual companion the renewed assurance of my affectionate regard.

Believe me, my dear Irving,

Always faithfully yours, ·

ALFRED AUSTIN.

Swinford Old Manor,
Christmas 1890.

DRAMATIS PERSONÆ.

LORENZO DE' MEDICI	*Ruler of Florence.*
BARTOLOMMEO SCALA	*His Chancellor.*
PIER LEONI	*His Physician.*
PICO DELLA MIRANDOLA ANGELO POLIZIANO LUIGI PULCI	*His Intimates.*
PIERO DE' MEDICI	*His Eldest Son and Successor.*
CARDINAL GIOVANNI DE' MEDICI	*His Second Son: afterwards Leo X.*
BERNARDO DEL NERO NICCOLÒ RIDOLFI LORENZO TORNABUONI	*Partisans of the Medici.*
GIROLAMO SAVONAROLA	*Prior of San Marco.*
FRÀ DOMENICO FRÀ SILVESTRO	*Brethren of San Marco.*
PIERO CAPPONI	*An Influential Citizen.*
FRANCESCO VALORI	*Political Leader of the Frateschi and Piagnoni.*
MARCUCCIO SALVIATI	*Military Leader of the Piagnoni and Frateschi.*
DOFFO SPINI	*Leader of the Compagnacci and Arrabbiati.*

FRANCESCO CEI   .   } *His Friends and Associates.*
ANNIBALE SODERINI

LUCA CORSINI   .
DOMENICO BONSI .   .   .   } *Bigi or Ottimati.*
GUIDANTONIO VESPUCCI   .

FRÀ MARIANO   .   *A Franciscan Friar.*

CHARLES VIII.   .   *King of France.*
PHILIPPE DE COMINES .   } *In the King's Suite.*
MARÉCHAL BEAUCAIRE .

LUDOVICO SFORZA : *Il Moro* .   { *Uncle of the nominal Duke of Milan.*

BETTUCCIO   .   *A Poet.*
NICCOLÒ GROSSO   .   *An Artist.*
CANDIDA DONATI .   *A noble Orphan.*
LETIZIA .   .   .   *Betrothed to Bettuccio.*
ANITA .   .   .   *Wife of Grosso.*

THE SIGNORY.   THE DIECI DI GUERRA.
THE OTTO DI BALÌA.

CITIZENS.   COMPAGNACCI.   ARRABBIATI.
FRATESCHI.   PIAGNONI.   MONKS.
A CRIER.

TIME :—*From April 8th* 1492 *to May* 23d 1498.

NOTE.

The *Piagnoni* or Whimperers, and *Frateschi* or followers of
the Friar, were both adherents of Savonarola ; but, while the
former were more especially his religious or pious followers,
the latter were distinguishable rather as his political adherents,
and friends of popular government.

The *Compagnacci* or Roysterers, and *Arrabbiati* or Furious Ones, were both opposed to Savonarola, and in about an equal degree from their dislike of his austere teaching and of his political tendencies.

The *Bigi* or Greys, and *Ottimati* or Aristocrats, were one and the same : oligarchs who held in aversion the supremacy of the Medici, the religious enthusiasm of Savonarola, and government by the people.

ACT I.

SCENE I.

[The chief apartment in the Medicean Villa at Careggi, built for Cosimo, " Pater Patriæ," from the designs of Michelozzi, and the favourite retreat of Lorenzo de' Medici.   Through an Italian window, which stands open, can be seen the city of Florence, three miles distant ; the Cupola of the Duomo, the Campanile of Giotto, and the Tower of the Palazzo Pubblico, rising clearly into the air.]

BARTOLOMMEO SCALA, PICO DELLA MIRANDOLA, LUIGI PULCI, LORENZO TORNABUONI.   *Enter* PIER LEONI (right).

SCALA.

How is Lorenzo ?

LEONI.

Gallantly in spirit,
But with a subtle sluggishness of blood
That foils medicaments.   In other men,
When fever finds a lodgment, pulses bound,
And fire curvets through vein and artery.
But in Lorenzo's body it eschews

B

All customary channels, diving down
Through subterranean currents to the seat
Of sensitive existence.   He is like
Those flowers which in the summer of their bloom
Are dying at the root.

PULCI.

                    Out in your fears !
How would you have our princely prodigy,
Who ne'er in health resembled mortal men,
Be like them in disease?   He oversteps
All common rules.   What you conceive decay,
Will prove fresh efflorescence.   I will lay
My poems 'gainst your physic that he lives.

LEONI.

A generous wager ; but he soon may need
Nor Muse nor medicine.

SCALA.

                    What says Lazaro ?

LEONI.

My colleague of Ticino daily pours
Golconda down his throat.

TORNABUONI.

The whole of Ind
Were not too precious to save such a life.

LEONI.

To save it, yes! But lavish jewels are
As vain 'gainst death, within us, as without. .
Death gulps no bribes.

PICO.

The wolves were howling loud
All night above Fiesole, and gleams
Of intermittent light no fuel fed,
Flashed, ravaging the silence. Yesterday,
The caged Numidian lion rent his twin,
And roared for further havoc.

TORNABUONI.

And did you hear
The midday lightning smote the cupola
Of Santa Reparata, toppling down
Masses of masonry, bricks, metal, tiles,
Towards the palace of the Medici;
While simultaneously a golden ball
Dropped from Lorenzo's scutcheon to the street.

PULCI.

Is it the first time wolves were heard to bark,
Stones seen to fall?   Look!   O'er the April sun
An April cloud comes flying.   Shall I bid
Poliziano hug his amulet?

LEONI.

Be merry if you can.   I would I were!
But, though you mock at portents, where is he
That likes to see the weather change for worse
About the hour of noon?   Lorenzo now
Is in the just meridian of life,
When all man's various faculties should make
A marriage with each other; robust thews,
With a most delicate judgment; nimble brain,
With will impossible to move; a soul
To every air and motion sensitive,
Close wedded to a body, heat and cold,
Fatigue and indolence, and all the whims
Of outward circumstance unbudging leave
Alas! Lorenzo's immaterial part
From what he has substantial craves divorce

PULCI

O reconcile them quick, before the feud

Irreparable yawns.   Should Florence lose
A mastery so· mild, her course will be
Henceforth or sluggish or irregular.
His mind is like the rainbow, that bestrides
The earth with every colour, and hath rays
Beyond our seeing.   Government with him
Is but a graver gaiety, while sport,
By him led on, takes princely dignity ;
And like to Nature, whose device it is
To make a peace of all things, he includes
In his large self our petty contraries.

TORNABUONI.

But look ! he comes, with mildly lifted hand,
Accentuating wisdom to his son,
The young boy Cardinal.

PICO.

                        And, Scala, see
The other arm familiarly flung
Over Politian's shoulder.   Him he still
Loves best of all.

> [Enter LORENZO, (left), with POLIZIANO, and his son
>   GIOVANNI, a youth of seventeen, wearing the robes
>   of a Cardinal.]

LORENZO.

                    Good morrow, gentlemen !
I was upon a fatherly discourse
To Giovanni, which I can defer
If you have pressing matter for my ear.

SCALA.

No, pray say on !   Lo ! Florence smiles below,
And in her streets moves jocund Carnival ;
And whilst her mood is joyous, he who would
Another than Lorenzo's voice prefer,
Were folly's hopeless reprobate.

LORENZO.

                    Well, next
Remember this.   Be punctual as the sun,
Though others lag ; for deference sits on youth
Better than any garment.   Let your house
Be spacious more than splendid, and be books
And busts your most conspicuous furniture.
Buy gems for worth, not value.   Of your sire
Imitate nothing save his sober love
For the chaste lap of learning.   Feed your friends
With rare texts, not with banquets.   Friendship craves

The commerce of the mind, not the exchange
Of emulous feasts that foster sycophants.
Select for intimates, if such survive,
Men like to Pico and Politian.

PULCI.

And not like Pulci?

LORENZO.

Poet! be content
To have been loved by me.   He will require
No wit save wisdom.

[Turning to Cardinal GIOVANNI.]

But if you should meet
Large spirits like to mountain streams let loose,
Twisting this way and that, as if to make
Life's journey longer and more various,
Treat them indulgently.   Be not austere :
Outward austerity, as oft as not,
Is but the friar's serge 'neath which there lurks
More taste for sack than sackcloth.   For the rest,
Remember you are mortgaged to the Church
Without redemption.   Rome, not Florence, is
Henceforth your country.   But if you be wise,

Yourself will be the undiscovered link
To couple them together.   Where is Piero?

SCALA.

Playing *pallone* in the outer court.

LORENZO.

Playing *pallone !*

[Goes to the window, and gazes at Florence.]

O, how fair she looks !
There never was a kingdom like to that,
And kingdoms have been played away ere this.
Pray for your brother.

GIOVANNI.

So I do, that he
May lift his leading purposes aloft
As the sap rises.

LORENZO.

Ah, they tell me, trees
Shoot only just as high as they dive deep ;
And much I fear his shallow-rooted soul
Will soar but dwarfishly.

SCALA.

The Commonwealth
Hath made herself the sponsor for your debts,
As you for hers responded.

LORENZO.

Welcome news !
Yes, I have been a spendthrift for the sake
Of my fair Florence, proud that she should wear
The splendour that hath beggared me.

SCALA.

So now
We must perpend what impost to prefer.

LORENZO.

Well, have a care to tax men tenderly.
For if you pilfer all the eggs at once,
You'll find the nest deserted.   Take but one,
To-morrow will another fill its place.
What news from Pisa ?

SCALA.

News that doth not change.
Pisa still chafes against your government.

LORENZO.

Then let the medicine, like the ill, not change.

'Tis fear unseats the horseman,—not the horse.

Touch his proud stomach with a rowelled heel,

He'll know a master rider.

POLIZIANO.

                              Yet there comes

From Pisa, dear my master, such a gift

As in your eyes submission will outweigh.

Roscio of Pisa found and sends you this.

> [He points to a bust of Plato, which stands on a pedestal,
> and which he, PICO, PULCI, and TORNABUONI have
> been examining.]

LORENZO.

What ! Plato's bust, in feature as he lived !

Pisa for this must wear a looser chain.

How noble and familiar he looks

'Twixt Scipio and Faustina !   The great gods

Are still at home in any company.

But how about the Pandects?

PICO.

                              All but done ;

And then unto the Codex.   Martial's text

Prospers apace in Calderino's hands,
While Fontio tackles Persius.

LORENZO.

                        All were well,
Could years revive like learning !   I would fain
Make Florence wise even as she is fair.
But this activity we boast hath bounds,
And all the running waves of eager life
End on the motionless fixed strand of death.

PULCI.

Savonarola sermonises thus.

LORENZO.

An easy way of preaching ; you do well
To drag me upward from this drowning vein.
Half the reputed wisdom of the world
Is but the lack of sane sagacity
To lay the ghost of sorrow.   But what news
Is current of the Prior of Saint Mark ?

TORNABUONI.

He makes a widening conquest of men's hearts,

And occupies them solely. Frà Mariano
Scatters in vain his honied homilies;
The flies have ta'en to vinegar.

LORENZO.

A sour-souled monk! He came into my house,
And never asked for me. And when that I,
Not to be foiled in courtesy, repaired
Unto his convent garden, he, 'twould seem,
Was busy with his prayers. Gifts he disdains,
Confronting them as bribes, forgetting, though,
To send me back the library, the busts,
And all the antique fragments that my House
Have squandered on his thankless monastery.
Well, well, from Heaven when men credentials bring,
They often treat this poor earth scurvily!

TORNABUONI.

I would have sent him long since to the Court
Whose arrogant ambassador he is.
What doth he here in Florence? You should raise
A wind about his ears to set his cowl
Towards Ferrara. Hard at prayers indeed!
His exhortations trespass on the State;

His sermons are sedition glibly faced
With a veneer of piety.   He lights
The flame of disaffection in men's minds.

LORENZO.

Beware, lest if you blow it out too hard,
You blow it in again.

SCALA.

                    Sir, I have sent
Valori, with four intimates, to mind
This pulpit-politician of the laws.
Have I exceeded my authority?

LORENZO.

A seasonable message ne'er is ill.
But, for your choice, Valori is a vane
For every wind to play its whimsy with ;
And the slim arrows of his wit will veer
Under the friar's gusty arguments.

PULCI.

Besides, I have suspected latterly,
Valori is indifferently drawn
Towards your rule, since you forbade him mate

With the lone orphan the Donati left,
The dainty Candida, who lulls her grief,
They tell me, with the mortuary drone
Of Frà Girolamo.

LEONI.

How comes she, in sooth,
To be so dainty?   For a sorrier pair
Than sire and mother alike, I never drugged.

LORENZO.

Is then your science, doctor, left at fault?
Know, Nature, like the cuckoo, laughs at law,
Placing her eggs in whatso nest she will;
And when at callow-time you think to find
The sparrow's stationary chirp, lo! bursts
Voyaging voice to glorify the spring.

PULCI.

Softer she be, the harder sure it seems
For him that must forego her.

LORENZO.

Wherefore hard?
Why, look but on the first hedge-rose you meet;

'Tis lovelier much than any maid alive,
And is far more encased in innocence.
Its breath is sweeter, and if it should fade,
Well, you may pluck another.   But a maid,
That you have once dissevered from her stem,
Upon your breast for ever must you keep,
Though all the scent of love evaporate,
And leave you but the stalk of what she was.

POLIZIANO.

Is then this Candida so wondrous fair?

TORNABUONI.

Fair as the world when yet 'tis hardly Spring,
But swelling buds and purpling coppices
Admonish it is coming.

LORENZO.

                    There/ replied
The close-observant lover!   Happy you
Lorenzo Tornabuoni! for none else
Shall wear this vernal blossom on his breast,
Till moist Spring wax to Summer's parching heat,
To Autumn's too material fruitfulness,
Then wintry disillusion.

PULCI

　　　　　　　Back you glide
Into your sombre vein, traducing thus
The hues of life.

LORENZO.

　　　　　Life's a chameleon,
Whose colour is fit argument for fools.
But let us all to Florence, and defeat
These monkish menaces with merry songs,
Minted to mark the reign of Carnival.

　　　　[Suddenly he totters, and stretches out his arm. CAR-
　　　　DINAL GIOVANNI and POLIZIANO are swiftly at his
　　　　side, and LEONI approaches.]

LEONI.

Feel you amiss?

　　　　　[LORENZO recovers, and puts them gently aside.]

LORENZO.

　　　　　No, nothing.　There!　'Tis gone!
" Flower of the clove !"—How, Pulci, goes the strain ?
Hence! hence!　Come, Pico!　Come, Politian!
Learning must now join hands with levity,
And foot a jocund round.　We all must go,
Yes, you as well, my solemn Chancellor,—

All, saving Giovanni.   Cardinal,
Keep gravity engaged till we return.
We shall be back to Vespers.

        [They all prepare to leave.]

GIOVANNI.

        Fare you well !
And I will go refresh myself with work,
From the fatigue of too much idleness.

SCENE II.

PIAZZA OF THE DUOMO ; THE FAÇADE, AND THE CAMPANILE
OF GIOTTO, AT THE BACK OF THE STAGE.

[Enter a Carnival Procession of both sexes, the most conspicuous
figures among which are DOFFO SPINI, ANNIBALE SODE-
RINI, and FRANCESCO CEI (right).   All are running and
romping.   Some are masked, others not, but all are richly
or fantastically attired.   Many carry baskets of flowers,
with which they pelt each other and the passers-by.]

SPINI.

Now let us sing the song Lorenzo made
The year his daughter Maddalena wed
The Holy Father's son, Francesco Cibo.

SODERINI.

Hush ! Holy Fathers have no children, boy ;
You mean his nephew.

CEI.

Have it as you will.
Are we not all his children ?   Now, the song !

[They wind round the stage, singing the following song,
     and pass out gradually (left).   Enter NICCOLO
     GROSSO and his wife ANITA (right).]

I.

Now comes Spring with buxom pleasures,
    Buds and sunshine, dance and song ;
Gallants, foot your friskiest measures !
Maids, unlock your daintiest treasures !
    Youth and springtime last not long.

II.

Every wall is white with roses,
    Linnets pair in every tree ;
Brim your beakers, twine your posies
Kiss and quaff ere April closes ;
    Bloom and beauty quickly flee.

ANITA.

Not a new gown to honour Carnival !
When not the basest citizen but pours
His purse upon the pavement for his wife.

GROSSO.

Mine is already empty.   Look at it !

      [He draws his leathern pouch from his girdle.]

ANITA.

Then why not swift replenish it ?   Your hands
Hang idle, while Lorenzo stretches his,
Imploring you for statues, miniatures,
Busts, anything you will.

GROSSO.

          And do you think
I, for Lorenzo, will my art demean
To make him more magnificent ?

ANITA.

          Others do,
And all their wives walk finely.

GROSSO.

Fie on you !
What would you say, were I to bid you hire
Your beauty out to use, and urge you to it
By argument from others?   Sooth, your gown
Is well enough

ANITA

And am I beautiful ?

[She approaches and caresses him.]

GROSSO.

How you have caught the blackbird's homely pipe,
Now sweet, now scolding !

ANITA.

Better mate, I ween,
Than is the lark that only sings in Heaven.

GROSSO.

Make thyself Heaven, and I will sing to thee.

ANITA.

Ah ! to do that, I needs must go far off,
Or thou wilt ne'er think me celestial.

GROSSO.

Then go and trim our nest upon the ground :
I am not always singing.   But before
You homeward wend, this wisdom in your ear
Why do you come betwixt my Art and me ?
In that, you are as foolish as the Earth,
When it thrusts in between the sun and moon,
And gets the light of neither.   This eclipse
Bars me from art, and leaves you solitary.
Pass, and let each in turn illuminate
Your giddy round.   Well, you shall have the gown.
Choose it as much like me as possible,
Who now am but a remnant, going cheap.

ANITA.

Dearer to me than any younger piece,
My gifted artist !   Hark !   Again they come,
The gaudy revellers.   I straight will hie
And make my beauty yet more beautiful.

> [Exit (left). Re-enter Carnival Procession (right), singing,
> dancing, and playing practical jokes. With them,
> BETTUCCIO and LETIZIA, hand in hand, whom they
> salute with flowers and pleasantry ; GROSSO, with
> folded arms, looks on.]

III.

Toss the hay and scent the clover,
Chase coy damsels till they trip.
What is life when life is over?
While it lingers play the rover,
Play the bee to honeyed lip.

IV.

Soft cheeks blush and dark eyes twinkle,
Bosoms swell with light desire ;
Ankles twitch and bracelets tinkle,
Love and joy smooth out the wrinkle ;
Death is smoke, let youth be fire !

[The Carnival passes out (left).]

GROSSO.

Ho ! pretty maiden, will you sit to me ?

BETTUCCIO.

To you, good sculptor ! She's my model now.

GROSSO.

How ! When for marble did you quit the Muse ?
I thought you were a poet.

LETIZIA.

So he is,
And I am sworn to marry him.   His song
Hath made love liquid ; he melts pearls of speech
I' the bubbling wine of a young maiden's blood.

GROSSO.

Nay, marry not a poet.   He will have
As many changeling mistresses as moods.
He wantons with the February winds,
And toys with March's forward daffodils.
He is an April fool each cuckoo-call
Can set a-gaping, and he falls in love
With every lamb that frisks its pretty tail.

LETIZIA.

He may love all, so that he loves me too.
Who would monopolise a poet's heart,
Large as the universe ?   It is enough
To sit within it.

GROSSO.

May you never find
Its vastness cold.   But, meanwhile, warm yourself.

         [Exit GROSSO (right).]

BETTUCCIO.

Heed him not, sweet! the wisdom of the world
Is far too general; we poets are
Diverse as our detractors.

LETIZIA.

Be it so!
We women, when we love, are all alike.
Go like the sea and like the sea return,
Thou still wilt find me here.   I am thy shore,
That slopes towards thee, and knows no other bent.
Nor will I ask if any fickle moon,
Swaying thee hither and thither, thy motions rule.
Smile on her as thou wilt and she on thee;
But thou must never so unfaithful prove
As to withhold the burden of thy moan,
When nights are dark and heaven untenanted,
From my deep-anchored lap.

BETTUCCIO.

I'll never leave it,
Though every star in heaven should shine on me.

[Re-enter Carnival Procession (left), singing, dancing, and
joking. BETTUCCIO and LETIZIA stand aside, hand

in hand.　At the same moment SAVONAROLA appears on the steps of the Duomo, accompanied by FRÀ DOMENICO, FRÀ SILVESTRO, and other monks.]

SAVONAROLA.

What do you here, you Pagan roysterers,

Roaring around the pillars of God's House

Your lewd fantastic canticles!　The Sword

Hangs by a thread and is about to fall,—

To fall, ay, and on Florence.　Put off quick

Your carnal garments, and make haste to don

The sackcloth of repentance, triflers all,

That, Christians called, are worse than infidel,

Blasphemers, usurers, slaves to fleshy lusts,

Mortgaged to Hell, whom Christ would fain redeem.

Blessëd are they that weep!　You only laugh.

Shameless as Sodom are ye, and as deaf,

Seeing no star in the East!　Accursëd be

Your obscene songs and foul frivolities!

Accursëd they that writ and they that sing,

Accursëd in their offspring and their doom!

The Sword of the Lord is sharpened, and your necks

Shall feel the smiting of its edge.　How long,

How long shall I implore you, Florentines!

My voice is hoarse with calling, and my tongue
Cleaves to my mouth, and none is there that hears.

BETTUCCIO.

Look! in resplendent trim Valori comes,
With Bonsi and Vespucci in his train,
Luca Corsini likewise hurrying up.
We shall see sport directly.

> [Enter FRANCESCO VALORI, LUCA CORSINI, DOMENICO
> BONSI, and GUIDANTANIO VESPUCCI. SAVONA-
> ROLA turns towards them.]

        Likewise you,
Who should uphold the Commonwealth and be
The solid buttress of the State, are but
Lorenzo's sycophants.

BETTUCCIO.

      Who blasphemes now?
Cheers for Lorenzo! Come, my lads and maids,
Convince this kill-joy friar that your lungs
Have not gone dry with singing canticles.
Long live Lorenzo the Magnificent!

ALL.

Long live Lorenzo and the Medici!

VALORI.

You hear them, friar? They use plain arguments.
But I with gentler messages have come,
Commissioned by Lorenzo to lament
You use him so distrustfully. Other sons
Of Dominick, when lifted to the rank
Of Prior of your Convent, homage paid
To him their benefactor; but you flout
His pious gifts, and fling them in his face.

SAVONAROLA.

You count them gifts, I reckon them as bribes,
And have rejected them accordingly;
And as to my election, that I owe
Not to Lorenzo, but to God alone,
And unto God I pay my fealty.
May that be all?

CORSINI.

   Your answer is as rough
As smooth was his remonstrance. We are charged,
If failing in our embassy, to warn,
Still in respectful language, there are laws
That give disturbers of the city's peace
But choice of exile or obedience.

SAVONAROLA.

Go tell Lorenzo that it is not I
But he that will be exiled ; exiled too
Unto a land whose exiles ne'er return.
Before the unrising Judgment-Seat of God
I summon him, Lorenzo ; after him,
Shortly, Pope Innocent ; and swiftly then,
King Ferdinand of Naples ; and this Three,
To God must answer for the swinish trough
That Italy doth wallow in.   The cup
Of her abominations now is full,
Full unto overflowing.   Tell him that.

BONSI.

You are ungracious, Frà Girolamo !

SAVONAROLA.

God is ungracious, when men spurn His grace.
But you, Valori, in whose heart I glance,
You will be left to serve a nobler work
Before you die.

BETTUCCIO.

And, Friar, what of us,

My sweetheart and myself?   Not every day
One gets one's fortune prophesied for nought.

SAVONAROLA.

The fountains of felicity run dry
When youth's no more in season.   I will keep
A girdle and a hair-shirt for you, boy;
You yet may need them.   Meanwhile, hold her sweet,
And from her heart divert all bitterness.
Come, brothers Dominick and Silvester,
We'll to our Convent.

> [Exeunt (right) CORSINI, BONSI, and VESPUCCI.   SAV-
> ONAROLA and Monks retire into the Duomo.
> The Carnival revellers break out again into merri-
> ment.   A girl throws a rope of flowers round
> LETIZIA.]

GIRL.

A girdle for Letizia!

SECOND GIRL.

And behold
A hair-shirt for Bettuccio!

> [She tries to put a sack over his head.

BETTUCCIO.

Peace, you romps!

And pray you tell us, sir, if to our sports
Lorenzo be not coming.

VALORI.

                          'Tis the hour
He should be from Careggi on his way,
With a most gallant company.   His friends
Are at the gate by this.

BETTUCCIO.

                          Then let us hie
Unto San Gallo, there to welcome him,
Fast followed by yon other stream of joy
That flows this way.

ALL.

                    On for San Gallo, on !

[They all pass out (left).   As they do so, a fresh Carnival
    Company, headed by SODERINI, enters (right), teas-
    ing and chasing CANDIDA, who seems scared, and
    rushes to VALORI for protection.]

VALORI.

My pretty bird, how fast your bosom beats !

[To the crowd.]

So roughly you a fledgling should not chase.

SODERINI.

We did not plan to hurt her.   She's so shy,
And with her foolish fleeing tempts pursuit.

CANDIDA.

[Still confused and alarmed.]

Forgive me, sir, for clinging to your arm ;
But they were me importuning with words
I do not understand, but much mislike.
But oh ! 'tis he !

[She breaks away from VALORI.]

VALORI.

Yes, maiden, it is I ;
Who would protect you with these living hands,
If death were your pursuer.   But why leave
So swift the port where you a shelter found ?

CANDIDA.

They mean no harm.   It was a foolish scare.

SODERINI.

My comrades, hence !   Lorenzo else will miss
The welcome you intend him.   This coy maid
Hath found a bold protector.   Thus it is :   ;

The timid creatures call aversion fear,
But danger which they love, security.

[Exeunt SODERINI and the revellers (left).

VALORI.

How gracious Fate hath been to me to-day,
Driving your fears this way !

CANDIDA.

Not gracious more
Than unto me providing at my need
Such valid help.   I thank you, and farewell.

VALORI.

The hunted hare stops longer in her seat
When the tormenting greyhounds have swept by,
And found another scent.   Stay just awhile,
Until the trepidation of your heart
Subside to gentler rhythms.

CANDIDA.

So it has.
My heart again beats temperately now.

VALORI.

Alas ! alas ! too temperately far !

But as the snug earth thaws the wintry snow,
Thy very coldness keeps my love so warm
That it must surely end by melting thee,
And make those icy lids and frozen orbs
Windows and eaves of dripping tenderness.

CANDIDA.

O sir ! I pray you do not talk of love.
My heart is in the grave, my hope in Heaven,
Where my dear parents have preceded me,
Taking life's summer with them.

VALORI.

                              Say not that !
Grief in young hearts is like the nightingale,
Whose note is almost sweeter than 'tis sad,
And stays but briefly.   Then when he is gone,
The cuckoo calleth lustier than before,
Proclaiming loud his victory of joy.
So, sweet, sad maiden, will it be with you.

CANDIDA.

There's silent winter now, silent and bare :
I have gleaned happiness.

D

VALORI.

Let hopeful love
But drive its furrow through the fields of death,
There yet will wave a harvest; but, if not,
Lend me your desolation, and we twain
Will still be sad together.

CANDIDA.

You forget.
If I could more than filial fetters wear,
For other chains Lorenzo destines me.
You speak of love and liberty to one
Who lacks the second even as the first.

VALORI.

Can you give one, the other being denied?

CANDIDA.

In the old lore of love I am not skilled.
But hearts need not be erudite to know
If love be sweet, compulsion must be sour,
And other maidens say that love is sweet!
I have not tasted it.   But hark! they come.

[There is the sound of returning Carnival.]

VALORI.

Nay, do not go !   I will protect you still.
Or, ere you go, tell me that love *is* sweet.

CANDIDA.

Sweet as a rivulet one stays to hear,
Yet doth not know its meaning.   Be my friend.
Friendship, 'tis said, is love without his wings,
And friendship, sir, is sweet enough for me.

VALORI.

But I would rather be your love than friend,
For see, it follows, I could fly to you.
> [Enter Carnival Procession (right), headed by BET-
> TUCCIO, followed by LETIZIA ; also ANITA, in her
> new gown.]

VALORI.

Why, stripling rhymester, back again so soon ?

BETTUCCIO.

Ill news, ill news !   Lorenzo hath not come.

ANITA.

But he *must* come.   What think you of my gown ?

BETTUCCIO.

You should have bought it black.　　Lorenzo's eye
Will never fall upon your finery.
They say he's dying.

CANDIDA.

　　　　Let us go and pray
That he may live.

VALORI.

[To Candida.]

Pray for the obstacle
Of all I yearn for !

CANDIDA.

　　　Hush !　Love should at least
Be silent in the corridors of death.
Farewell !

VALORI.

　　Farewell !　But this, to take away.
Though from my lips thou may'st remove thine ear,
Withal, as in some sea-suffusëd shell,
The ocean of my love shall murmur still.

　　[Exit CANDIDA (right).　Enter (left) FRÀ DOMENICO and
　　　　FRÀ SILVESTRO.]

FRÀ DOMENICO.

Go home ! go home !   Lorenzo's hour hath come !
Lorenzo, master of your revels when
Life sat upon his heart and waved his plume.
Now death hath mounted up behind, 'twere meet
You should suspend awhile your carnival.

VALORI.

But surely, friar, Lorenzo is not dead ?

FRÀ SILVESTRO.

Not dead, but now so tightly clutched by death,
That he hath sent for Frà Girolamo
To loose his soul.

ANITA.

No use then in my gown.
I would that I had waited.   I must go
And pray them change it for a funeral one.

                              [Exit ANITA (left).]

LETIZIA.

Savonarola's prophecy hath quick
Marched to its issue.

FIRST GIRL.

Ay, and look you, child,
He prophesied about Bettuccio's fate.

SECOND GIRL.

And wove a hair-shirt for your wedding night !

FIRST GIRL.

Yes, and a girdle, but not one of love.

VALORI.

My friends ! it were more seemly to depart,
Since this grave news looks true.   Lorenzo dead
Would shame your revelry ; and should he live,
He will remember with due thankfulness
You put on gravity in time of joy,
Because he was not joyous.

CROWD.

True !   Very true !
'Tis just what we were going to say, ourselves.
So let us separate.

BETTUCCIO.

Then come, Letizia,

And we will be as glum and miserable

As love will let us.

[They all prepare to depart.   The scene shifts.

SCENE III.

[The same as in Scene I., at Careggi ; but a curtain is drawn
     across the stage, cutting off the interior of the apartment.
     Enter (left) PICO DELLA MIRANDOLA and LUIGI PULCI.
     At the same time enter (right) LEONI.]

PULCI.

What news, physician ?

LEONI.

News most ominous.

Lorenzo, not contented to be shriven

By his own confessor, Matteo Bossi,

Nor by Frà Mariano, hath besought

That Frà Girolamo will hither come,

And ere he journey to the other world,

Arrange his soul.

PICO.

The Prior of Saint Mark's,
Savonarola !

LEONI.

Even he in sooth.
He will be here anon.

PULCI.

You stagger me.
But often so it is : the steadiest souls
Seem to lose equilibrium when they stand   ·
Upon the narrow edge that doth divide
This life from the deep precipice of death.
I had not thought it.

PICO.

Doth he suffer much ?

LEONI.

He must, though his brave visage still belies
The stomach's agonies, to which the gout,
Routed from limbs, hath sulkily retired.
He gleans no comfort from our tepid baths
Nor Bono Avogradi's heliotrope.

PULCI.

Are we to lose him then ?   Alas ! alas !
The loftiest leaves are blown away the first,
While lowlier foliage melancholy hangs
Through half the winter !

> [POLIZIANO appears from behind the curtain, and draws
> it back.   LORENZO is seen reclining on a couch at
> the back of the stage, near the window overlooking
> Florence.]

POLIZIANO.

Lorenzo craves his dear familiars
To come as near him as they are in thought.
Will you approach ?

LORENZO.

                    Come close, Mirandola !
I could not die contented save I had
With thy young aspect first refreshed myself.
Learning and loveliness in thee have paired,
And seeing thee once more, I take farewell
Of all I lived for.

PICO.

                    You are ruddier now.
Dismiss death's far too early messenger,

And bid him come again at stroke of age:
Give him not audience yet.

LORENZO.

                Death hath no hours,
But makes his own appointments.   Better so:
For, Pico, I am out of heart and breath,
And could not breast the hill of life again.

POLIZIANO.

But what a height, my master, you have climbed!
And if the moment to descend have come,
Survey once more the conquered territory,
And die believing that no mountain soars
So loftily as that aspiring name
That you will leave behind.

LORENZO.

                Consoling thought!
But, O Politian! if our labours live,
It will but be as tablets on a tomb
For sake of those that they commemorate,
Our names no more than speaking monument
To tell the world where a great spirit lies;

And we shall borrow from dead Plato's dust
What pinch of immortality we keep.

PULCI.

To Plato generous, why be thus unjust
To his posterity?   Lorenzo's age,
Poised on its own broad pinions, shall defy
The downward gusts of time, while weaker wings
Are whirled beneath the horizon.   Tongues unborn
Shall lisp the sweet survival of your deeds,
As children practise with a father's name
To learn a larger utterance.

LORENZO.

                              Spoken well,
And worthy of my poet.   But this vein
Of forward-reaching vanity infects
Each generation, this one most of all.
Nought new is said, but only newly thought :
And these pretentious novelties wherein
The upstart age struts proudly, are but gems
Carefully carven by an older time,
Now furnished with fresh setting.

POLIZIANO.

[Aside to PICO and LEONI.]

Hark how he talks !

Too equably for one that is to live.
Only when death over our shoulder leans
And guides our childish fingers through life's page,
Write we in such well-balanced characters.

LORENZO.

[Raising himself on his elbow.]

I want you all to hold in tenderness
Hieronymo Donato, Barbaro,
And Paolo Cortese, for my sake.
You know how they have traversed land and sea
To help me bridge the present with the past,
And open out for penetrating minds
Unexplored lands of learning.   See you too
That Giovanni Lascaris, whose freight
Of twice one hundred volumes, ransacked fresh
From cloisters of Mount Athos, hath been sucked
Down by the ignorant waves, doth not receive
Less than the promised guerdon had he brought
That argosy to shore.

PICO.

It shall be done.
Myself will see to it.

LORENZO.

Pulci, to you
I do commit my poesies that have
Enjoyed obscurity.

PULCI.

They quick shall greet
The light that waits for them.

LORENZO.

No, Pulci, no!
Consume them utterly.   I would recall
Much that is now on every Tuscan tongue,
If that were possible.   Our Plato held
The Muse should sing but praises of the Gods
And hymns to virtue.

PULCI.

You on me put a far more murderous task
Than I have heart for.

LORENZO.

                Friendship orders you.
Hark to the thrush gurgling in yonder tree!
He hath inhaled the liquid air whilst flying,
And, now he chooses him another perch,
Gives it us back in notes intangible;
Which is the very music that we want,
Did we but know it.   For your spoken song,
Too full of meaning, lacks significance.
Hark how again he sings celestially,
The very heaven of music meaningless!
He is a better poet than us all.

> [An attendant enters (left), and whispers to Pico, who is
> joined by the rest.   They confer silently, while
> Lorenzo gazes out towards Florence.]

LORENZO.

Does your debate concern me, gentlemen?

POLIZIANO.

The Prior of Saint Mark is now without.

LORENZO.

Then let him come within.   He is a guest

That I have need of.   Go, divert yourselves.

With him I must hold dialogue of death

Before life's curtain falls.

> [They take tender leave of him.   Exeunt (right).]

LORENZO.

[Alone.]

My intimates !

The best men ever had, but helpless now

To hold me here or cheer me thitherward.

Of all the company of hearts that sit

Round our existence smiling, that not one

Should be told off to see us to the land,

The road of which we know not !   That seems hard.

To be alone in the full glare of life

Lulls fear to sleep.   But loneliness in death

Might make the most intrepid spirit take

Shadows for substance.

> [The door (left) opens, and SAVONAROLA appears.   He
>   stands pausing in the doorway.   LORENZO motions   .
>   to him to approach.]

SCENE IV.

SAVONAROLA.   LORENZO.

LORENZO.

Will you approach, good Prior?   'Tis not from lack
Of reverence for your habit, that I fail
To greet you more becomingly, but death
That glues my limbs.

SAVONAROLA.

[Advancing.]

> No need to rise, Lorenzo.

Heaven lays no tax of courtly ceremony;
But, being far more exorbitant, it claims
Full payment of the substance from the soul.
Why have you sent for me?

LORENZO.

> To readjust,

Before I journey on, unbalanced wrongs
That gall my conscience.

SAVONAROLA.

                        Show me them !
Since that it seems Plato avails not now.
Philosophy, like any false ally,
Comes to man's aid when need is at the least,
To shrink away in true extremity.
But Virtue, unaffected friend, contrives
To pull us through, though all the fiends conspire
To wedge us in with evil.

LORENZO.

                        I have made
Elsewhere confession of my homelier sins.
But those transgressions that have walked abroad
In all men's eyes, I have reserved for one
Who knows no private favour.

SAVONAROLA.

                        Then speak on !
Death is the looking-glass of life wherein
Each man may scan the aspect of his deeds.
How looks it now, Lorenzo, now that God
Holds that unflattering mirror to your soul ?

LORENZO.

'Tis hard on twenty years since, but still, still,
The cry of sacked Volterra haunts my ears.

SAVONAROLA.

And well it may, Lorenzo!   Do you think
Thus to divide eternity?   Twenty years
Have placed no second 'twixt your sin and you.

LORENZO.

I know it, Prior; and poignantly confess
To you and Heaven the guilt was mostly mine.
Endorsing claims equivocal to glut
The yawning coffers of the State, I clutched
A shadowy right; the alum mines were won,
And now the gain lies leaden on my breast,
Though bade I not the slaughter.

SAVONAROLA.

                              Hold!   We bid
Whatever buttresses our bold designs,
And are the architects of every wrong
Raised o'er the ruins of demolished right.
You cannot take before the throne of God

The quarry of your hunting; but the blood
Clings to your hands.

LORENZO.

               Seem they so very red?
So red, contrition cannot wash them white?
For there is other gore that soaks my skirt,
Spilt in usurious payment of the blow
Struck by the Pazzi at my life, but spilt
Not from vindictiveness but policy.

SAVONAROLA.

Will policy avail to change the score
Of the Recording Angel?   Hell is full
Of politic expedients, condoned
By Earth, to double their offence 'fore Heaven.
God saved your life; you slew your enemies.
               [LORENZO exhibits signs of agitation.]
Yet will He pardon even as He saved,
So anguish in the balance lift up guilt.
Is your confession ended?

LORENZO.

               Alas! no.
Full many an orphan maiden hath been robbed

Of dowry guaranteed ; and virtue, shorn
Of its substantial outwork, hath succumbed
To the besieger.   This seems direst wrong——

SAVONAROLA.

And is the direst wrong.   The body pushed
Out of this life precociously may find
A better tenement.   But he that fouls
A virgin soul and leaves it to corrupt,
Would strain God's mercy to the snapping-point,
If it were not far-reaching as Himself.
You must amend this injury.

LORENZO.
                    Show me how,
And quickly will I do it.

SAVONAROLA.
                    'Tis enough.
Let restitution be in full ordained ;
And, if you live, each victim ferret out
And wed her to the cloister.

LORENZO.
                    Doing this,

May I the Almighty Arbiter confront,
And reckon on indulgence?

SAVONAROLA.

     Nought that is,
Mountain, nor sea, nor the vast atmosphere,
Nor even man's stupendous scope of sin,
Can get beyond the circumambient range
Of Divine mercy.   But before my hands
May absolution shower upon your soul,
Three things there are first indispensable.

LORENZO.

What may these be?

SAVONAROLA.

    Firstly, that you should have
Faith in God's mercy, living faith and full.

LORENZO.

And that I have; for if I had it not,
How ill-caparisoned were I to start
Upon this final journey!

SAVONAROLA.

Next, that you
Make reparation absolute, and lay
This as a prior legacy on your sons,
For lingering wrong to friend or enemy.
To this you pawn your soul?

LORENZO.

My soul be bond,
And forfeit if I fail!

SAVONAROLA.

Lastly, Lorenzo,
But mainly this of all, you must restore
Her liberties to Florence.

LORENZO.

[Starting forward on the couch.]
Friar, hold!
You overstep your territory there,
And make a raid on my dominions.
Remember what is Cæsar's.

SAVONAROLA.

Do I fail?
Where did you get your empire? Who was it gave

The Medici on Florence that sly grip
Which you have tightened?   Nay, invoke not God!
For he as Cæsar ne'er anointed you ;
And, failing His anointment, show me then
The sanction of His people.

LORENZO.

What I have,
They freely gave.

SAVONAROLA.

They were not free to give ;
For you with splendour first corrupted them,
Drugging their love of virtue, that you might
Their love of freedom violate, and they
The detriment discern not.

LORENZO.

I gave all,
All that I have, all I inherited,
To vivify this city, and to lift
Her diadem of glory high above
All cities, kingdoms, principalities,
Lavished the substance of my House on her,
Discriminating not which hers, which mine,

And die with empty coffers that enriched
The fame of Florence.   Was it crime in me?
In face of heavenly ermine will I claim,
For that, exemption.

SAVONAROLA.

    Pandars might as well
Plead the foul price they pay, as you invoke
The substance squandered on the Commonwealth,
Whose freedom you have ravished.   Well you know
In Florence that the government of One
Was an abomination till your Line
Drew all the reins of rule into its hand,
And jingling trappings of subjection laid
Upon a pampered people.   Glory!   Fame!
Fame is but sound; conscience makes harmony;
And happy he who truthfully can say,
When the world's pagan plaudits cease, he hears
The sacred music of a virtuous heart.
Give Florence back her freedom!

LORENZO.

      She *is* free,
And of her freedom made me what I am,

And by that freedom will unmake my sons
If they run short of wisdom.

SAVONAROLA.

　　　　　Then, enough !
And summon your attendants.

　　　　　[LORENZO rings.　His friends enter.]

　　　　　You have need
No more of me.　But this, Lorenzo, mark !
What you refuse, that Florence swift will take,
When your magnificence shall lie entombed,
And God arraign you for the rights you filched,
But could not carry with you, nor bequeath.
Die, by my voice unshriven !

　　[His friends crowd round him.　SAVONAROLA turns to
　　　　depart, but pauses, and gazes at LORENZO with a
　　　　look of austere menace.　Curtain falls.]

END OF ACT I.

ACT II.

SCENE I.

[The Piazza della Signoria : the main entrance to the Palazzo
Pubblico at the back of the stage, and the Loggia de'
Lanzi on the right.]

SPINI, SODERINI, CEI, COMPAGNACCI.

SPINI.

I tell you what, my comrades, you must work.
There's little to be earned by merriment,
Since great Lorenzo died.

FIRST COMPAGNACCIO.

      Work! I'll not work :
It is a turnspit's task.

SODERINI.

      Faith ! then you'll starve :
A leaner task than turning any spit.

SECOND COMP.

Wait till the French King comes.   I wager, then
There will be food for fooling.

CEI.

                        Fools for food,
Will prove more like.   Which of you has not heard
His infantry in fight not only fell
But slay their enemies?

FIRST COMP.

                Uncivil boors !
They will learn gentler ways in Tuscany.

SPINI.

They're mighty slow at learning, then.   The blood
Shed at Rappallo was but Magra's stream
Compared to Arno's, with the torrents loosed
At Fivizzano.

SECOND COMP.

Why, they're monsters !

SODERINI

                                    Ay,
Monsters in stature, appetite, and lust.

They ravish first, and rifle afterwards.
Upon the hale they wreak their savagery,
Then fall on the unarmed.   They covet blood,
But ransom more.   Your jewels, caskets, gems,
Velvets, embroideries, satins, silks, brocades,
All to their gullet stands for provender.
They think the stones of Italy, if sucked,
Will yield them oil; so meagre is their land,
So fat is ours.

CEI.

Neither do courteous wiles
Disarm their greed.   When Blanche of Montferrat,
Wearing her costliest jewels, on behalf
Of Savoy's Prince, because a minor still,
Proffered a gracious welcome to their King,
He took the precious gewgaws from her neck,
And for ten thousand ducats pawned them straight.

FIRST COMP.

I've got no jewels.

SPINI.

But you've got a neck;
And, failing necklaces, your neck will serve.

SECOND COMP.

Zounds ! that it will.

SODERINI.

I know Rappallo well,
Perched on the lap of olive-crested gorge,
And safely smiling at the smiling sea,
Till these ferocious foragers of death,
With swords for sickles, reaped each standing life,
Ripe or unripe, then gleaned the hospitals
For further slaughter.

FIRST COMP.

But what wants this king
In Italy at all ?

CEI.

Why, just what kings,
Since crowns first turned their heads, are wont to want,
A bigger stage to strut on.   This one claims
The fief of Naples.   Florence has to choose
Whether to show a front or lend a side.

SPINI.

Hither comes one, to tell us more of this,

Marcuccio Salviati, with his kin :

A Piagnone, but an honest man.

How doth the slip of such a sturdy stock

Come to be bent by Frà Girolamo?

> [Enter SALVIATI (right), followed by a number of Piag-
> noni, all dressed soberly, but some of them, like
> himself, armed.]

What news, Salviati, of the Commonwealth?

SALVIATI.

The latest, Piero hath betaken him,

With Gianfigliazzo and Giannozzo Pucci,

Unto Sarzana, to the French King's camp,

To sue for terms for Florence.

FIRST PIAGNONE.

      Sue for terms !

A pretty suitor ; barbarous, uncouth,

His mother's son.

SECOND PIAGNONE.

    But half a Florentine :

Expert in midnight broils and secret loves

A hero at *pallone*, passing on

All serious business to his Chancellor,
Ser Bibbiena.

SODERINI.

Who is there denies
He is not like Lorenzo?   'Twere in vain
You asked the duplicate of such a Prince.
But he's Lorenzo's son, a Medici,
And that's enough.   Whom would you have to stand
At top of Florence?

FIRST PIAGNONE.

Better none than he.
Our Frà Girolamo's a likelier man.

FIRST COMP.

Savonarola!   A Dominican!

SECOND COMP.

A monk!   A vagrant from another world!
The pulpit is his place.

SPINI.

A place from which,
Worse plague upon 't! already he directs
The hearts of half of Florence.

SALVIATI.

And ere long
Will guide them all.   Pico, Politian,
Each in the garb of Domenick expired,
By him absolved.   Say, did he not foretell
That the French King would come, and in the face
Of reputable citizens predict
Death to Lorenzo and Pope Innocent,
And Ferdinand of Naples last of all?
And each is gone.

SODERINI.

A holy prophecy!
That robs us of Lorenzo, and exalts
Roderigo Borgia to St. Peter's Chair,
Thanks to the mule-loads of ill-gotten gold
Into Ascanio Sforza's palace driven
At time of conclave.

FIRST PIAGNONE.

That was not the work
Of Frà Girolamo.   But yesterday
He thundered in the pulpit of Saint Mark
'Gainst the election simoniacal
Of the new Pontiff.

SPINI.

Whereby he invents
Fresh enemies for Florence.   Pious work !

SALVIATI.

The enemies of Florence are within.
Who is there pleads like Frà Girolamo
For restitution of our ancient rights ?

PIAGNONI.

And we will have them.

OTHER PIAGNONI.

Have them, that we will.
Down with the Medici !

[Enter (left) LORENZO TORNABUONI.]

TORNABUONI.

Down, down, yourselves,
You sniggering whimperers, hangers on the skirt
Of an officious shaveling ! Clasp your palms,
And mumble litanies, or flog your flesh !
But dare to meddle with the Commonwealth,
There are who will convince you of your place.

F

SPINI.

Ay, that there are, and quickly.

> [The two parties, the COMPAGNACCI and the PIAGNONI,
> lay their hands on their swords, and assume an
> attitude of menace towards one another. SALVIATI,
> by gesture, seeks to calm the PIAGNONI.]

SECOND PIAGNONE.

Heed them not,

Lascivious brawlers! Let us bear their jibes,

And prove our Christian humility.

FIRST COMP.

So very humble : humble as your monk,

Who sets himself above the Signory,

And——

> [Enter SAVONAROLA (left), accompanied by FRÀ
> DOMENICO and FRÀ SILVESTRO.]

SAVONAROLA.

Brethren! Citizens! Why, what is this!

Is this a time for Pagan acrimony,

When round your city adversaries throng

Dense as lean wolves in wintry Apennine?

Have I not warned you that the Church, and not

The Church alone, but equally the State,
And most this State of Florence, will be scourged,
And renovated next, and that ere long?
Hear yet another vision.   In the night
I saw a hand in Heaven, and in the hand
A sword upon whose steel was brightly chased,
"The Sword of the Lord over the earth, swiftly and
     soon!"
And many voices heard I, plain and clear,
Promising mercy to the good, but loud
Stripes and confusion menacing to the ill,
And clamouring that the wrath of God is nigh.
The air grew pitchy dark, and thickly rained
Swords, lightnings, spears, and fiery javelins.
Rumbled the thunder, and the whole earth lay
A prey to battle, famine, pestilence.
Then, ere the vision vanished, came a voice
Commanding me to frighten you with fear,
And prophesy fresh scourges.   Hear again!
The Sword of the Lord over the earth, swiftly and soon!
'Tis imminent to fall, nor can you get
Beyond its smiting.   O convert you quick,
Beseeching God to stay His ire and send
True pastors who may win back vagrant souls.

The sword of the Lord ! the sword of the Lord ! I say,
Swiftly and soon !

TORNABUONI.

     And who commissioned you
Such scourges to invoke ?   If Florence feels
The trembling of the air a sword divides,
Who bade the French King swoop down Apennine,
And hover o'er this city?   You are leagued
With Ludovico il Moro to inflict
Upon us this invasion.

SAVONAROLA.

     To foretell
Is not to fashion.   I but prophesied;
And have not these my prophecies come true?
Lo! I will bring the waters over the Earth!
And over the Earth they are coming!   Yet why fear?
Enter the Ark, all ye who will: its doors
Stand open still.   Let all of you be quick,
For coming is the time they will be shut,
And who then stand outside the Ark of God,
Will smite their breasts in bootless penitence.
Yes! the New Cyrus comes, God's Scourge he comes,
And all who will repent not shall be scourged.

The prophecies are verified, the Sword
At length, at length is here !   Over is the time,
Over, O Florence, the time for dance and song,
And in its stead hath come the time for tears.
Thy sins, O Florence ! and thy sins, O Rome !
O Italy ! thy sins, this scourge have caused.
How often have I clamoured in thy ears,
How often wept, O Florence, that my voice
Might yet suffice thee !   Unto Thee, O Lord,
To Thee, to Thee who died for us, I turn !
Pardon the people of Florence who would fain,
Though tardily, be Thine !

TORNABUONI.

[Interrupting him.]
And why should they

Be spared, and others spared not?   You have lured
A curse to Italy, and now would waive
The mischief from our heads !

SALVIATI.

And he will do it.

FIRST PIAGNONE.

Trust him, he will, and Florence will be spared.

SECOND PIAGNONE.

Hush, man !   He's going to prophesy again.

SAVONAROLA.

And who is man, to argue with his God ?
Hath not the potter power upon the clay,
. And of the self-same lump may he not make
That vessel to dishonour,—honour this ?
Tell me, O Magdalen ! why now you dwell
In Paradise, who sinned as even we ?
Why, Peter, who on Tabor's Mount beheld
Your Lord transfigured, yet denied Him thrice
Shamefacedly to lowly handmaiden,
Why do you now beatitude possess,
And yours the headship of God's Church ?   Thy sins,
Thy many sins, are all forgiven thee,
Since thou from alabaster vase didst pour
Unguents, and on His feet repentant tears.
Not for thy merits, Magdalen ! and not
For thine, O Florence, art thou privileged,
But that God loves and favours whom He will.
Pray, and give alms, or else the sword will fall !
Hence to Saint Mark's, to Vespers !

> [SAVONAROLA, accompanied by FRÀ DOMENICO and
> FRÀ SILVESTRO, crosses the stage, the COMPAGN-
> ACCI making way for them. Exeunt (right), followed
> by SALVIATI and the PIAGNONI. BERTUCCIO mean-
> while has entered, and remains behind with TORNA-
> BUONI, SPINI, and the COMPAGNACCI.]

SPINI.

You see the drift he has upon their wills.

They speed along like leaves before the wind,

And only halt until he blows again.

TORNABUONI.

More reason that our breath be timely spent

On things less volatile.   Paolo Orsini

Hath left for Lucca, in obedience

To orders from Piero.   In his place,

Keep an unwinking eye upon the Gates :

These Whimperers mean mischief.   Hence at once ;

And while they pray, do more effectual work.

SPINI.

Come, Soderini, Cei, comrades all,

We now have occupation.

> [Exeunt SPINI and COMPAGNACCI (left).]

BETTUCCIO.

                              With your leave,
I too, sir, will depart.

TORNABUONI.

                    Unto your love ?
O happy swain, that like the shepherd's star
Are in the evening just as near the sun
As in the morning.

BETTUCCIO.

                    · Prettily conceived : ˗
But you wrong both with your comparisons
She is the star, and follows in my wake,
Although I be no sun.   She shines afar
Of her own lovingness, and makes the dark
Glow like the noon, and distance feel as near
As though I touched it.

TORNABUONI.

                    Ah ! I plain can see
You see her plain, although I see her not.
Where is she now ?

BETTUCCIO.

With me, in verity :
Ostensibly with Grosso, whose fine touch
Hath begged her for a model.

TORNABUONI.

And you lent !

BETTUCCIO.

Lent willingly.   'Twere churlish to refuse.

TORNABUONI.

Is she then such a model, round and round ?

BETTUCCIO.

She hath no other merit save to love ;
But this one virtue so transports her sex,
That all her faults are lifted from the ground,
And nothing foul can touch her.

TORNABUONI.

Hath she wit ?

BETTUCCIO.

Just enough wit for apprehending mine.

She is the sap and would not be the tree,
Moves like the leaf nor wants to be the wind:
Insensibly and passively she lends
Her motions to the instincts of assent,
And spends her freedom in obedience.
You spoke of stars.   See you, 'tis not a chain
That makes them one same centre circle round,
But faithful parallels; they, but for these,
Would rush against each other or apart.

TORNABUONI.

Still may to you all stars propitious be!
They love me not.

BETTUCCIO.

   It is my low estate
Makes my security.   Were I like you,
Noble, esteemed, conspicuous in men's eyes,
The coyest and most shrinking joy there is
Might fly me too.   I'm a poor poet, sir!
Cheaply reputed, yet so dearly loved,
That if you thrust your rapier through the Earth
Till it protruded on the other side,
You would not fathom it; and so, farewell!
Prosper in your ambitions!

TORNABUONI.

Stay, sweet youth ;
For the ambition warmest in my blood
Is but to be as happy as you boast.
I love the Lady Candida, but she
Confronts me icily.   Now the fair maid,
Who is your shadow, is her shadow too.
I mark them much together.

BETTUCCIO.

They are twin.
But have you never noted, when a maid
Is in the first strange flow and flush of love,
She oft will lavish on the passive form
Of some near maid the fond experiments
Her instinct is too maidenly to prove
On our responsive selves ?

TORNABUONI.

You poets mark
So many things in women that we miss.
But I would fain you said an honest word
To this your sweet, that she in turn would say
An honest word for me to—well, you know—

To her who is more sweet to me because
I yet have tasted but her bitterness.

BETTUCCIO.

I your ambassador will be with zeal.
But from Letizia latterly I heard
That, save for Frà Girolamo's assent,
This comely orphan would her tresses clip,
Frame her young forehead in a plaitless veil,
And at her girdle hang a rosary.

TORNABUONI.

Is it she may the better fly from me?

BETTUCCIO.

Vex not yourself.   Whatever maids affect,
Tends but one way.   Clasp they a crucifix,
'Tis that there are no baby lips to kiss.
Their prayers are sighs, their vows most virginal
But a deep need for tenderness and tears.

TORNABUONI.

But why doth Frà Girolamo divert
Her footsteps from the cloister?

BETTUCCIO.

                              Who shall say?
Methinks he favours the Valori's suit,
As I will favour yours.

TORNABUONI.

                         Well, go and suck
The sweet that waits you.

                    [Exit BETTUCCIO (right).]

                         There are thousand lips
'Twixt Bellosguardo and Fiesole,
Ripening for harvest, that I too might reap,
But keep my sickle for a churlish soil,
And starve amid abundance.   Hither come
Del Nero and Ridolfi.   They will wean
My pursing lips from bosom that runs dry.

               [Enter (left) DEL NERO and RIDOLFI.]

SCENE II.

TORNABUONI. DEL NERO. RIDOLFI.

TORNABUONI.

What tidings from Sarzana?

DEL NERO.

                              None as yet.
Save Ludovico's gird when Piero craved
Excuse for having missed him on the road:
" One of us two hath missed his road, 'tis plain,
But 'tis not I, I warrant."

RIDOLFI.

                              Much I fear
The gird was true.   Purblind in confidence
While the French King yet dallied by the way,
Now that the lazy gonfalons of Charles
Unfurl and flap towards Florence, Piero makes
Obeisance forward.

DEL NERO.

No worse policy.
How otherwise Lorenzo snatched the State

From imminence of peril, fronting full
A foe declared, yet knitting friends betimes,
Making a turncoat of fixed fate itself,
And outmanœuvring mightiest menaces.
Would he were living now!

TORNABUONI.

Yet we must stand
Fast by the son, that by the father stood.
I never will desert him.

RIDOLFI.

Softly, boy!
Who hinted at desertion?   But, if one
You pluck back from a precipice should plunge
Over its edge, would you still follow him?

TORNABUONI.

No; but 'twere well, lest Piero's foot should slip
Through mere mischance, like daring mountaineers
To rope ourselves together.

DEL NERO.

So we should,
If he in desperate ventures were expert.

But far from risking on the slippery height
Of absolute contention all he hath,
Lo ! he goes crawling to the French King's camp,
And seeks his safety in glib lowliness.
Already potent Ottimati, like
Bonsi, Corsini, and Vespucci, join
Their hands with brawling levellers, to run
His pennon from the mast-head of the State.

RIDOLFI.

And have you noted in the public streets
Men of unwonted steadiness of eye,
And handling weapons of another time,
Such as Michele Lando and his band
Of carders brandished ninety years ago
In this same Florence ?

DEL NERO.

        Likewise the great Guilds
And Crafts of Industry are all astir,
Foremost among them those of wool and silk.
There's mischief manufacturing.

TORNABUONI.

            Sure enough.

And can I cast a ravel in their skein,
Trust me to do it.

RIDOLFI.

              You will be well employed ;
Better, by far, than lavishing your breath
In the vain chase of a maid's tortuous whims.

TORNABUONI.

The circle of her beauty draws me in.

RIDOLFI.

Then have a care it does not drag you down.
Fie on you, boy !   Women should never be
More than the narrow margin of our life,
Past whom its text runs on continuously.

TORNABUONI.

A truth more promptly ta'en to head than heart.

DEL NERO.

Yet, fervent youth, bear it in memory !
Nor struck there ever timelier hour than this
For purging fancy's sedentary sighs
With draughts of action.   Take it from me, boy,

G

There's no such physic for the love-sick soul

As the brisk air of public policy.

The Signory have summoned in hot haste

This evening a Grand Council.   You be there,

As will I and Ridolfi.   Fare you well,

Until the Council be convened.   How short

Churlish November cuts the genial day !

RIDOLFI.

Under long nights conspiracies can hide.

TORNABUONI.

Be it ours, then, to uncloak them.

> [Exeunt DEL NERO and RIDOLFI (left).   Enter CANDIDA
> and LETIZIA (right).   They do not observe
> TORNABUONI.]

CANDIDA.

Yes, to-night,

After the Council.   When the stars are high,

We'll roam together.   Mind you fail me not.

LETIZIA.

There never offered the occasion, sweet,

Of sunning me in your warm gaze, but I

Was quickly perched there.   Until then, farewell.

[LETIZIA exit (right).   CANDIDA turns to cross the stage; and, after advancing a few steps, sees TORNABUONI, and halts.]

TORNABUONI.

Think of the angels !   For of you I thought
That very instant !   But is instant none
I do not think of you.

CANDIDA.

                    Sir, think no more
Of one so little worthy of your thoughts.

TORNABUONI.

'Tis I that am unworthy, well I know,
To house so rich a guest in my poor mind.
But you have entered there and must not quit.
I'll try to furnish it with noble thoughts,
So that you may not feel a stranger in it.

CANDIDA.

No need to furnish it anew for me.
With nobleness it is already stocked ;
And, by that nobleness, I beg you will
Keep it——well, not for me.

TORNABUONI.

                            If not, for whom?
Surely we are betrothed?

CANDIDA.

                            O sir! by whom?
By one who never had the power to bind.
Lorenzo mated us for policy,
I never yielding even mute assent.
Be noble, and forget me!

TORNABUONI.

                            Hath the will
Power over memory?   I shall forget
When all I am pales to oblivion,
But not before.

CANDIDA.

                Then think of me as one
To whom you inclined graciously and got
Best reverence in return.   There! let us part.

        [She is going to pass him, but he bars the way.]

TORNABUONI.

Not in this wise, and never in this world,

Unless it be some other have secured
The prize I wrestle for.   Tell me out plain:
Is your heart yours to give, or is't enslaved
Unto Valori?

CANDIDA.

Sir, I think you fail
Somewhat in courtesy.   My heart is Heaven's:
No earthly tenant yet hath entered there;
Nor, saving you, hath any sought to force
His way in without knocking.

TORNABUONI (*aside*).

That is why
They stand without.   No chaste maid lifts the latch.
But open it yourself, they lack the strength
To thrust you forth!

[He draws nearer to her.]

Your hand was placed in mine.
Lorenzo plighted us, and that pledge I
Sealed with my melting love, as now I stamp
Myself upon your lips.

[He kisses her by force.   Enter (right) SAVONAROLA,
FRÀ DOMENICO, and FRÀ SILVESTRO.]

SAVONAROLA.

Lorenzo Tornabuoni !   What is this ?
A noble maiden ! you, not noble less,
Outrage her modesty !

TORNABUONI.

> We are betrothed.

CANDIDA.

Pardon him, Frà Girolamo, as I,
Freely forgive.   But this, in right to me :
If it be true I plighted am to him,
'Twas by Lorenzo, shortly ere he died,
For public ends.

SAVONAROLA.

> Fie on you, sir, to claim
A bond like that, which Heaven's self hath made void,
Void in its sight before.   Go you, my child,
With Frà Silvestro : he will tend you home ;
Though I can read in every lineament
You have a guardian angel of your own.

[Exeunt (left) FRÀ SILVESTRO and CANDIDA.   SAVONA-
ROLA and FRÀ DOMENICO gaze after them.]

TORNABUONI (*aside*).

Curse on these shaven pates that claim to stand
Betwixt the soul and body!   But that kiss
Will sound her soul unto its very depths,
And fetch her up her secret.

[Exit (right).]

FRÀ DOMENICO.

See! he hath gone, nor waited to be chid.

SAVONAROLA.

His conscience chides him sharper than can I,
Or he had fled not.   Ah! how happy we,
The lawless ardour of whose fleshy lusts
In the cool cloister are extinguishëd.
But we must be indulgent to the heat
Of the unscreened world.   I do remember me
How at Ferrara, in my glowing youth,
A daughter of a Florentine exiled
From this contentious city, with a look
Transfixed my heart.   She was a Strozzi, but,
She not being born in wedlock, I conceived
His pride might stoop to me, a lowly youth;
But God, who loved me better than all love

Of man or maiden, kept me for His work.

They scorned me,—but enough.   Only, my son,

Love, if it happy or unhappy be,

Treat you indulgently.

FRÀ DOMENICO.

This maid would wed

The loveless pallet of a convent cell.

SAVONAROLA.

I know it; but 'twould be to injure Heaven

Did we the sad and sinking world deprive

Of such sweet household leaven, which should be kept

To make some good man's soul rise higher still,

And lighten his life's heaviness.   Come, my son !

We must go pray the Holy Spirit to be

With the Grand Council.

[Exeunt (left).   Simultaneously enter (right) SALVIATI,
accompanied by a strong band of armed PIAGNONI.]

SCENE III.

SALVIATI.

           Take care to stand your ground.
Spini and Soderini and their crew
Of Compagnacci come.   But never fear !
The people side with us, and all the Guilds
Have gone against the Medici.

> [Enter (right) SPINI, SODERINI, CEI, and the COM-
> PAGNACCI.   Then come on the processions of the
> various Guilds, and occupy the space between the
> COMPAGNACCI and the PIAGNONI.   The SIGNORY
> emerge from the Palazzo Pubblico, with the DIECI
> DE GUERRA, the OTTO DI BALÌA, and many leading
> Citizens, conspicuous among whom are CAPPONI,
> CORSINI, BONSI, and VESPUCCI.   They occupy
> the steps of the Palazzo Pubblico, and the Loggia
> de' Lanzi.   Citizens crowd in where they can.]

SPINI.

                      We are late.
Spread yourselves out.

SODERINI (*to some of the Compagnacci*).

                Remember, not to shout
Till Spini gives the signal.

CEI.

                              We shall wait
Vainly for that to-day.   'Tis plain enough
We are outnumbered.

FIRST PIAGNONE.

                    Lord ! how dark it grows !

SECOND PIAGNONE.

Yes, puzzling dark.   We must have torches.

SALVIATI.

                                        See !
Torches are coming.   Friends ! make room for them.

        [Men bearing flaming torches of grease and tow enter.]

CRIER.

Silence, good citizens ! that you may hear
Proposals from the Signory.

FIRST COMPAGNACCIO.

                    Look ! look !
Luca Corsini is about to speak.

SECOND COMP.

He is not the *Proposto :* Why should he
Break through the law ?

CORSINI.

              Dear fellow-citizens !
I am not the *Proposto*, neither hath
The Signory invited me to speak.
But times there are when, as the people know,
The people's safety is the highest law.

THE PEOPLE.

That's true enough.

CORSINI.

            And this is one of them.
Charles of Anjou, invited o'er the Alps
By Ludovico Sforza, hath affirmed
His claim to Naples, and with horse and foot,
Frenchmen and Swiss, some fifty thousand strong,
Hath fought his way unto your very doors.
But, fellow-citizens, he doth not come
An enemy to Florence ; only asks
A friendly passage.

A VOICE.

But our money too.

ANOTHER VOICE.

It seems that Florence always has to pay.

CORSINI.

Better to pay in money than in blood,
Which, when 'tis spilt, sucketh up money too.

VOICES.

There, he is right.

CORSINI.

Piero de' Medici,
Not heeding this, made of the King a foe.

[There is commotion in the Crowd, the COMPAGNACCI
    crying " No !" but they are shouted down by the
    PIAGNONI, the Guilds, and the People. CORSINI
    grows embarrassed. Young JACOPO DE' NERLI
    rises to back him up.]

NERLI.

Yes, made a foe who might have been a friend,
Whereby I tell you——

[There is fresh disorder. The father of Jacopo de' Nerli
    rises.]

FATHER OF NERLI.

Pay my son no heed :
He is too young, and of too crude a brain
To give ripe counsel.

[PIERO CAPPONI rises.]

VOICES.

Let us hear Capponi !
Capponi speaks !

CAPPONI.

Yes, fellow-citizens !
For I have words in me that will not wait,
But claim an exit.   Time is it to end
Our childish ways.   Piero de' Medici,
Unlike his father, bold yet politic,
Is ruining the Commonwealth.   He might,
As you have heard, have bargained with the King,
Who asked nought better.   But in lieu of this,
Partly from levity, in part from spite
'Gainst Ludovic of Milan, the King's friend,
He bade the Tuscan fortresses resist
The advance of Charles, who straight laid siege to
    them.
Know ye the latest tidings ?   Piero now,

Hastening in terror to the French King's camp,

Hath these your precious strongholds rendered up,

The keys of all our Tuscan territory:

Firstly, Pietrasanta, which to win

Florence a hundred thousand ducats spent;

With it Sarzana, which the State hath cost

Full fifty thousand florins; last of all,

Is Sarzanella.

> [There is again commotion in the Crowd, but it is
> manifest that the preponderance of opinion is
> against the MEDIÇI. CAPPONI goes on.]

Therefore I say once more,

Piero de' Medici is proved unfit

To guide the Commonwealth. Straight let us name

Ambassadors to Charles, who, if they meet

Piero upon the way, salute him not,

But to the King expound from whom it was,

From whom alone, proceeded enmity,

And that in Florence he and the French name

Have ever had and still will find a friend.

VOICES IN THE CROWD.

Truer he could not speak.

OTHER VOICES.

Say, could he?

OTHER VOICES.

No !

Long live Capponi !

CAPPONI.

　　　　　　　　Therefore we must choose
Men of repute and honour to convey
Our welcome to the King.　At the same time,
My fellow-citizens, we must not fail
To bring in from the country armèd men,
Trusty of purpose and discreetly led,
Who may within the city's unseen nooks,
Convents and cloisters, snugly be concealed.
And let not any Florentine omit
To have a dagger or a pike at need,
So that if this most Christian King demand
More than a splendid homage at your hands,
With 'chance some solid tribute which the French,
An avaricious race, love best of all,
You then may show him a fixed countenance,
In armour roughly-set.

　　　　　　　[The Crowd shout and clash their arms.]
　　　　　　　And now, my friends,
To choose Ambassadors.

VOICES.

We all choose you !

CAPPONI.

Good : I will go.   But there is one whose name
Is upon every lip, in every heart.
Know you that name ?

VOICES.

Yes, Frà Girolamo,
The Prior of Saint Mark !

CAPPONI.

Ay, none but he,
Savonarola, for he prophesied
The coming of the King across the Alps,
And who alone, nor I nor any one,
But only he, from Florence can avert
The ills invoked by Pier de' Medici.
Wish you that Frà Girolamo should go ?

THE PEOPLE.

Yes ! all—all—all—all of us wish it.

[The COMPAGNACCI are cowed and remain silent. Some
of them gradually slip away.]

CAPPONI.

To him I your election will convey.

He loves the people and will treat their choice

As though it were a message from on High.

And now, good citizens, disperse ; the night

Is deepening fast.   Hence to your homes, and trust

The Signory to save the Commonwealth.

> [The SIGNORY, the DIECI DI GUERRA, the OTTO DI
> BALÌA, and leading citizens, retire into the Palazzo
> Pubblico.   The Crowd gradually disperses, the
> COMPAGNACCI scowling at the PIAGNONI, and an
> air of suspicion and defiance pervading the multi-
> tude ; but no disturbance takes place. Meanwhile,
> the following dialogue goes on.]

SALVIATI.

Are you content Savonarola goes

To parley with the King?

PIAGNONI.

                    Ay, well content.

We all trust Frà Girolamo.

SPINI.

                    Hence, my friends !

We are outpolled ; but should it come to blows,

Sinews will count, not numbers.

> [Exeunt the rest of the COMPAGNACCI (left), and only
> BETTUCCIO and LETIZIA are left upon the stage.]

H

SCENE IV.

BETTUCCIO.   LETIZIA.

LETIZIA.

                      Here she comes,
As punctual as a star and yet more pure.

           [Enter CANDIDA (right).]

This is the lady Candida, whom I——

BETTUCCIO.

Praising so much, did not yet praise enough.

But I must leave you, momently to hie

To Tornabuoni, and apprise him quick

That matters march awry.   'Twas thought he would

Be present at the Council; but no voice

Could have withstood the torrent of discourse

That foamed 'gainst Piero.   Lady, with your leave.

      [LETIZIA embraces him.   He salutes CANDIDA, and
        exit (left).]

CANDIDA.

Is that your lover that you told me of?

LETIZIA.

None else.   What think you of him ?

CANDIDA.
                                            .

                                He is well,
And deft at courtesy.   But have a care
You love not overmuch.

LETIZIA.

                        That cannot be.
He is a poet, hence athirst for love,
And one must make a fountain of one's heart,
And keep it flowing.

CANDIDA.

                        What if it should well
When he would drink no more ?

LETIZIA.

                            O, you are wrong,
Echoing a common shout.   A poet is
The two extremes of our prosaic mean.
Because he gives so much, much he demands ;
No partial love contents him.   Being large,

He is not filled with little, but exacts
All that is in this tiny tenement,
And all it vastly longs for.

CANDIDA.

Happy youth,
To have found one woman in this cautious world
Who keeps back nothing!   Heaven scarce were
          Heaven,
To beggar this so prodigal a heart.
Yet have I heard that love was born a cheat,
And in the end will sweep up all your stakes!

LETIZIA.

That's when you play with him; a hellish game
No honest woman tries.   Bettuccio's long!
I wish he would return.

CANDIDA.

He scarce has gone.
You think your heart the clock, and that time ticks
With fancy's bounding pulses!   How I wish
That your Bettuccio had the grace to choose
A Cause as fair as you.   Why does he mate
With Frà Girolamo's worst enemies?

LETIZIA.

I never questioned him on such a thing,
Since alien 'tis to love.   Now, now I must,
Since I perceive that danger lies that way.
This Signor Tornabuoni was the friend
Of his convivial seasons in the days
While yet Lorenzo lived.   Men's amity
Is pledged above their beakers; and he vows
That braver gallant never kissed a cup.
He hath a noble port.

[Enter VALORI (left) breathlessly.   CANDIDA plucks
at LETIZIA's gown, to lead her away.]

VALORI.

Nay, do not go!
I am in need of some swift messenger.

CANDIDA.

None is more swift than I will be.

LETIZIA.

No, no!
You are too dainty for such common work.
Trust *me*, sir, with your message.

CANDIDA.

Both can go.

LETIZIA.

We must not ; for Bettuccio would return,
And neither find.

VALORI.

Now, fortune stand by me !
Speed, quick-fledged maiden :   I will stand on guard
By this fair lady while your errand runs.
Nor must I quit this place until you bring
Hither the Signory.   If in their beds,
Rouse them, and say Valori waits without.
Now quick into the Palace !   You must go
Round to the postern entrance.

[Exit LETIZIA (right).]

CANDIDA.

Sir ! you seem
To bear grave tidings.

VALORI.

Grave indeed they are,
But graver not to me than news that you
Could give me, an you would.

CANDIDA.

What may that be?

VALORI.

News, O, so long in coming!   Why do you live
Solitary as a swan and as content,
That, on some silent mere sedately moored,
Keeps turning on itself?   Yet lone swans have
Somewhere a nest.   Oh! make your nest with me,
Deep in the sedges of protecting love,
Where ripples of vexation die away
And winds are barred from coming!

CANDIDA.

With what ease
You ask what is with difficulty given!
You tell me that you love me.   That seems much.
If I love you, I do not know it, sir!

VALORI.

O, why do you delay in loving me?
The fruit that ripens slowly is half sour,
While sweetness comes with quick maturity.

CANDIDA.

Hush! or you'll wake the night!   Look at the stars,

Holding in Heaven their silent colloquy.
Why do they keep so silent?

VALORI.

Is't not because
Silence alone makes perfect harmony,
And in their concord ne'er a false note strikes
To scandalize the ear?

CANDIDA.

See!   One is falling—

VALORI.

Leaving a long trail.

CANDIDA.

Why doth a shooting star shine brightlier far
Than any that keeps fixëd in its seat?

VALORI.

'Tis, its career, being brief, is glorious.
Who would not into jaws of darkness jump,
Traversing first such bright trajectory?

CANDIDA.

Hush!   Falling stars are high examples sent

To warn, not lure.　Gross fancy says they are
Substantial meteors; but that is not so.
They are the merest phantasies of Night,
When she's asleep, and, dimly visited
By past effects, she dreams of Lucifer
Hurled out of Heaven.

VALORI.

　　　How sweetly moralised !
Where did you learn that wisdom ?

CANDIDA.

　　　At my prayers :
A fountain of instruction, much I fear
Men dip into but little.　You blasphemed,
So I made solemn your profanity.
Stars are the eyes of night, wherewith she sees
What ill we do, and silence is the ear
With which she listens.

VALORI.

　　　You are too pure a strain
To mix with my impurity.

CANDIDA.

That proves
You purer than you think.   If I could love,
It would be for the strong humility
That bends as low as I am.   See, they come.
Now lend your ear unto the State, nor brood
On private yearnings.   Florence wants your heart ;
Give it her wholly.

·VALORI.

At your bidding, yes ;
And she, when saved, will give it back to you.

[Enter LETIZIA (right), followed by CORSINI, BONSI,
and VESPUCCI.   CANDIDA and LETIZIA retire.]

VALORI.

Forgive me, gentlemen, for treating sleep
As though it were siesta of the day.
But I bear pressing news.   All goes amiss.

BONSI.

Come you from Pisa ?

VALORI.

Yes, from Pisa straight,
Spurring as fast as hoofs would carry me.

CORSINI.

Is the King there?

VALORI.

There, and with all his force
Whither the first Ambassadors we sent,
Unknown to Piero, now have followed him.

VESPUCCI.

But they found Charles at Lucca.

VALORI.

So they did;
And there the King showed reasonable mind.
But Piero, bidding higher, foiled their terms,
And now Charles craftily affects to treat
But with the Medici alone.

CORSINI.

Is 't true
That Piero hath contracted we shall pay
Two hundred thousand ducats?

VALORI.

So I learned,
Coming along the road. But hear you worse.

Not only Pietrasanta and the twin,
Sarzana, Sarzanella, are unlocked,
But Piero hath engaged to render up
Pisa.

ALL.

What !   Pisa !

VALORI.

            Yes, and with them too
Leghorn and Ripafratta.

BONSI.

            News the ear
Can scarce think audible.

VESPUCCI.

            And ne'er a tongue,
Unless it were Valori's, could announce,
And be believed.

VALORI.

         Alas ! 'tis positive !
And with it snaps the ultimate frail link
That tied me to the Medici.

CORSINI.

Yet stay !

What if against the city Charles advance,

Conveying Piero with him ?

BONSI.

Never fear !

Fool though he be, he hath the wit to know

That if into the saddle tilted back

By Charles or any other, Florence quick,

When these had gone, would buck him out of it.

He needs must grasp the stirrup for himself,

Or never mount again.

VESPUCCI.

He clutches now.

For the boy Cardinal who should have worn

The plain male garb of statecraft, and have left

The sacristy's adornments epicene

Unto this Piero, in his brother's cause

Works day and night through all the thoroughfares,

Lavishing gold, and plying still the cry

Of *Palle ! Palle !* but no echo finds.

[Enter (left) MARCUCCIO SALVIATI in hot haste.]

SALVIATI.

No palliation, gentlemen, I plead,
For breaking on your conference.   The news
I bring is my excuse.   Not one chime since,
Paolo Orsini, coming from without,
Seized on San Gallo Gate, and occupies
That quarter wholly.

VALORI.

Does he come in strength ?

SALVIATI.

Five hundred horse and twice as many foot,
And all the rabble shout for the Medici.

CORSINI.

That is the slum where still the vermin hide.

SALVIATI.

But 'tis believed Piero himself hath set
His face towards the city.

VALORI.

May it be true !
See, Salviati, that your trustiest hands

For no excuse disperse, and keep them near !
Apprise the Guilds.   I will not fail to lend
Assistance opportune.   The Signory
Will do the rest.

[SALVIATI retires (left).]

VALORI.

        'Tis patent, peril lurks
In this advancëd night, and will unfold
Its tokens with the dawn.   Who is 't to-day
Is the *Proposto?*

VESPUCCI.

      Intempestively,
Antonio Lorini, who commands
Likewise the Palace Keys ; so we took care
He was not woke.

BONSI.

      As care too will we take
Out of his hand betimes the keys shall slip,
Should they be wanted.

VALORI.

      Let us to our posts,
And sleep no more !   The night now nears its term,

And from its womb will issue forth a day

With freedom's chrism fair Florence shall baptize.

Valori ! be familiar with your sword !

[He draws his sword, and kisses the blade, then salutes
the three, and they all retire.]

SCENE V.

[Various signs of early morning. People living in the houses
in the Piazza open their windows, throw back the *per-
siane*, and look out. Artisans pass across the square.
Women come to the fountain with pitchers and brazen
vessels. Enter (left) SPINI, SODERINI, and CEI.]

SPINI.

San Gallo Gate is safely held, and there

Piero will find an entrance.

SODERINI.

As a rat

Doth to a trap that is to throttle him.

CEI.

Think you that, Soderini ?

SODERINI.

Faith ! I do.
All the Guilds go against us.   If it were
Only the Piagnoni showed their teeth,
Well, they might snarl ; but folk that know to bite
Have begun barking.

SPINI.

Is it true the arms
In the Bargello have been seized upon ?

CEI.

There's not a brat but brandishes a blade,
And blusters for the People.

SODERINI.

Look ! they stream
From every street and passage hitherward,
Clumsy with weapons.   We had best retire,
And keep our folk in hand.

[Exeunt (right).   People come trooping into the Piazza
    from all sides, armed with rusty swords, broken
    rapiers, old-fashioned pikes, etc.]

FIRST CITIZEN.

No work to-day, I warrant.

SECOND CITIZEN.

Deuce a stroke.

I've shut up shop.

THIRD CITIZEN.

We're all for Liberty.

Fine folks may wait for once : needle and awl
Must have a holiday.

FIRST CITIZEN.

They will be fortunate

If they get shaved.

TAILOR.

They're pretty sure of that.

Your barber is in wrangling times of peace
A valiant politician ; but the edge
Of his sharp wit grows blunt when risk's to shear.

COBBLER.

Ay, ay, your tailor is the likeliest man,
When clothes are to be torn.

TAILOR.

Save cobblers, who

Are useful when you want to run away,

And not to slip.

> [The Crowd laugh. Suddenly a noise is heard in the
> distance, and all of them rush towards the back of
> the stage, to see whence it proceeds. They give
> way as the sound gets nearer, and retire towards
> each side of the stage.]

FIRST CITIZEN.

It's Pier' de' Medici.

SECOND CITIZEN.

Hath he returned?

THIRD CITIZEN.

Look if he hasn't! with courtiers at his heels,

But courtiers with their forks out.

> [Enter PIERO, attended by his brother the CARDINAL,
> PAOLO ORSINI, and a goodly following of armed
> men.]

ORSINI.

Have you not got a cheer?   Hath garlic ta'en

The sweetness from your breath?

VOICES.

Down with the Medici!

We want no Medici!

ORSINI.

Want, or not want,
You'll have to bolt them.

> [ORSINI and his followers drive the people back, and
> overawe them. PIERO walks to the main door of
> the Palazzo Pubblico, and ascends the steps. As
> he does so the doors are thrown open, and the
> SIGNORY, headed by CORSINI, BONSI, and VES-
> PUCCI, appear in the doorway.]

CORSINI.

Piero de' Medici, what want you here?

PIERO.

To enter as I entered have before,
Whene'er I willed.

BONSI.

Your will no more is law.
You to King Charles would sell the Commonwealth
That is not to be bartered.

PIERO (*sternly, and attempting to pass*).

Leave, I say!
Pass through I will.

VESPUCCI.

Then through the postern gate,
Where others pass.

> [The CARDINAL and ORSINI rush forward to abet PIERO,
> but they are too late.   The doors are shut in
> PIERO'S face.   The Crowd take courage, and begin
> to hiss.   PIERO draws his sword, as though he
> would use violence against them.   At that moment
> the bell of the Tower of the Palazzo Pubblico
> begins to sound.   Fresh Crowds hurry into the
> Piazza, where reigns the utmost confusion, the
> people crying, "*Popolo e Libertà!*" "*Abbasso le
> Palle!*"   In the confusion, PIERO, still with sword
> drawn, retires, covered by ORSINI, the CARDINAL,
> and their followers.   TORNABUONI, RIDOLFI, and
> DEL NERO enter, followed by SPINI and the COM-
> PAGNACCI, who shout, "*Palle! Palle!*" "*Long live
> the Medici!*"   But VALORI, with an armed retinue,
> appears, and the party of the MEDICI gradually
> retire, till the stage is occupied only by the PIAGNONI
> and the People, who shout, "*Popolo e Libertà!*"
> TORNABUONI, DEL NERO, and RIDOLFI linger;
> and a CRIER appears on the steps of the Palazzo
> Pubblico.]

CRIER.

Five thousand florins will be paid to him
Who Pier' de' Medici brings here alive,
Or Cardinal Giovanni; and, if dead,
Two thousand florins.   This the Signory

Promises solemnly, and thus proclaims
Both rebels and both outlaws.

:[Enter SALVIATI.]

SALVIATI.

An offer made too late.   Pier' de' Medici
Passed through San Gallo Gate, and spurs him fast
On to Bologna, in the company
Of his brother Giuliano.

THE PEOPLE.

Libertà !

Popolo e Libertà.   Down with the Medici !

VALORI.

Hence to the *Podestà*, and drag we down
The effigies placed there by Cosimo
In '34 ; and with them those that look
From the Dogana gate, more recent trace
Of rule to be obliterated now !

[Exeunt VALORI and his retinue, followed by the
People.]

RIDOLFI.

How light these new keels run before the wind !

Let us but help them with a following breath,
They will capsize.

TORNABUONI.

I rather would confront
Their giddy course and send them staggering down,
Than lead them forward.

DEL NERO.

You were best in port
Until this hurricane shall cease to blow.
Follow an old man's counsel, and depart.

TORNABUONI.

That, if I must.　But never will I catch
A watchword from their greasy mouths and smack
My lips upon it; so, for now, farewell!

[Exit TORNABUONI (right).　Enter SALVIATI (left)].

SALVIATI (to DEL NERO).

Sir, you had best go crouch.　The people gut
Your son Antonio's hearth; the like they do
To Giovanni Guidi, and no less
To Antonio Miniati.　Passing on

From Via Larga, where they sacked the house
Of the young Cardinal, they plunder now
His treasures in the garden of Saint Mark.
Your turn will surely come.

RIDOLFI.

      Then let us hide,
While yet is time.

  [DEL NERO and RIDOLFI prepare to depart ; but the
    populace enter again from different points, crying
    " Abbasso le palle !" DEL NERO and RIDOLFI
    shout *" Popolo e Libertà !"*]

FIRST CITIZEN.

Ha ! here they are !   And harken how they shout
For Freedom, as the devil brought to bay
Mouths Scripture.

SECOND CITIZEN.

     Let us make an end of them !
They are enemies to the people.

THIRD CITIZEN.

        No, not death,
But only fire.   Hence let us to their homes !

VOICES.

Yes, yes!   We'll teach these lords of privilege
What freedom means !

> [SAVONAROLA, attended by FRÀ DOMENICO, FRÀ
> SILVESTRO, and other Monks, suddenly appears on
> the Piazza.]

SCENE VI.

SAVONAROLA.

　　　　　Hold ! Christians ! Florentines !
What wickedness is this ?   Hath the Lord God
Delivered you from tyranny of One,
Only to let this city undergo
The tyranny of Many ?   Truce henceforth,
Truce to vindictiveness !   God spares who could
Crush all His enemies ; you too must spare.
The Medici have gone, have fallen, have fled,
And all the meretricious gauds of power
Have brushed your Gates.   Down on your knees and
　　give
Thanksgiving unto Christ who liberates,

And liberated you.   The French King comes ;
And how will you receive him if your hands
Be black with burning Christian hearths ?   Forbear,
As ye would be forborne with.   Know, the Scourge
Hath not yet passed.   The Sword of the Lord still
          hangs
Aloft in the sky.   Would ye avert it, show
Mercy to the unmerciful.   No more blood,
And no more fire, but prayer, and love, and peace.
Shortly you will be summoned to pronounce
On your new Government ; but no more blood nor fire,
Nor ransacking of roofs !   Florence is free,
And Christ is King !   Clamour ye loud for Christ,
Now and henceforth King of the Commonwealth !

THE PEOPLE.

Long live Christ !   Long live the Commonwealth !
Long live Savonarola !

SAVONAROLA.

Now await
The entry of King Charles with mingled mien
Of Christians and of freemen.   As a friend
He comes ; a friendly welcome lend to him.

The Scourge of the new Cyrus shall descend

On other walls than yours, if carnal toys

You put away, and mortify the flesh,

Indulged so long.   Now once more, Long live Christ !

> [The People again shout as SAVONAROLA bids them,
> and gradually disperse.   He too retires, followed
> by his Monks.   Enter GROSSO (right), followed by
> his Wife.]

GROSSO.

Rate me no more.   The artist's mind should brood

On its intention long and silently ;

But you so often lift me from the nest,

My purpose cools, and that which might have been

Matured to punctual perfectness, when hatched

Is part abortive.

ANITA.

Keep your simile,

To mend yourself.   You never are on cluck,

Unless the fair Letizia be at hand

To clap you to a sitting.   Why should she

Be indispensable the more than I ?

My bust is shapelier far than hers, my arm

More ripe and rounded.   She is raw and lean.

Her daintiest charms are locked against your gaze,
At least they ought to be, and shall be, too,
Whilst mine are at your bidding.

GROSSO.

                              True, good wife.
But Art is less material than you deem,
And gloats on the invisible.   Besides,
This maiden sits so patiently, she lends
A sympathetic instinct to my touch.
She never rails at me, but smiles as sweet
As fresh-culled spray of dewy eglantine,
Whose blossom, pinky-white, is half unclosed,
Half shut upon itself.

ANITA.

                              She flatters you,
Plain with her tongue, yet plainer with her eye ;
And men with adulation can be caught
As easily as flies with syrup are.
Thicker and coarser that the mixture be,
The more they stick.

GROSSO.

                              Then why not try that way,
To hold me fast ?   My duty is to you,

Likewise my wont.   But never doubt of this:

My fancy wanders unrestrainedly,

Alighting upon all things fair and sweet,

And with what sugared bounty they secrete

Stocking invention's hive, that cannot live

On one sole flower, howe'er with honey brimmed.

If this be infidelity, I am

The most unfaithful vagabond alive;

And so rail on.

> [Exit ANITA, in dudgeon (left).   Enter SALVIATI and
> PIAGNONI (right).]

SALVIATI.

Come on, my fellows, we are here in time

To pick the choicest standing-ground, nor lose

One word of wisdom by our elders dropped.

There!   Range you so!   Ho, Grosso!   Is it you?

Have you, too, come to hear the tough debate

Between the Frenchmen and our Signory?

GROSSO.

Not I, in sooth.   There's talk enough at home

Without resorting to the market-place.

Argue away; I will retire me where

Time is not squandered in vain controversy,
But what I think, I do.

       [Exit Grosso (left).]

    FIRST PIAGNONE.

     That gentleman
Thinks not thin wine of himself.

   SECOND PIAGNONE.

      Which of them does?
These transcendental artists in the end
Idealize themselves.

     TAILOR.

     I often thank God
I was not born a sculptor.

     COBBLER.

    Nor a poet.
They are worst of all.

    [Enter Spini and Soderini (right).]

     SPINI.

    A merry time you'll have,
Now that the Medici have gone.   The French   .
Are chalking all your doors.

FIRST CITIZEN.

What! Have they come?

SODERINI.

Thick through San Frediano Gate they stream
And eddy where they will.

COBBLER.

I think I had best
Go home and see what's doing.

SPINI.

Better not:
You may see more than caution bargained for.

COBBLER.

I think I'll go. 'Twere wiser.

TAILOR.

Faith! not I.
My wife will guard the hearth.

SODERINI.

But who'll guard her?
These friends invoked by Frà Girolamo

Have ta'en no monkish vows.   A slender waist
Decoys them even from a rounded purse.

SECOND PIAGNONE.

Heed not his gibes; he is a partisan
Of Piero, lately taken to his heels.

    [Exeunt (left) COBBLER and TAILOR, the Crowd laugh-
        ing and jeering.]

SPINI.

But not, like you, and your smug sniggering kin,
Ally of these transmontane pilferers.
We are for Florence.   Here is one that brings
The greenest news.
                  [Enter CEI (left).]

FIRST PIAGNONE.

      What tidings have you, sir?

CEI.

Tidings quite good enough for such as you.
The Pisans have revolted, and the King
Lifted no hand to stay them while they drove
The Florentine Commissioners away.

SECOND PIAGNONE.

Then Pisa's lost!

SODERINI.

Lost, just as we shall lose

Town after town to gratify your spite

Against the Medici.

THIRD PIAGNONE.

’Twas Piero’s self

Was willing to surrender it.

[Shouts are heard in the distance, and more people enter
the Piazza.]

SPINI.

Hark! what now?

SALVIATI.

A rumour grew that coming with the King

Was Pier’ de’ Medici; and all the streets

Straight teemed with citizens.   But now ’twould seem

’Tis but his wife and mother that appear

In Charles’s tail.

PIAGNONI.

Orsini, aliens,

Not Florentines at all!

SECOND CITIZEN.

But who are to treat
With the French King?

FIRST PIAGNONE.

Why, Frà Girolamo.

CEI.

Always this monk!   Capponi, happily,
With your heaven-born diplomatist is yoked
Likewise Valori; with them Bonsi, skilled
In endless embassies; and last, Vespucci
Whose mind is lined with parchments.

SPINI.

But what says
Charles of Anjou, with whom they have to treat?

SODERINI.

Ever the same reply: that everything
Will be arranged when once he finds himself
In the great city.

[Enter fresh Crowds.   A CRIER appears.]

CRIER.

Give place, gentlemen !

The Signory are coming to receive

Charles of Anjou.

> [As he speaks, the SIGNORY, the OTTO DI BALÌA, the
> DIECI DI GUERRA, and the four Commissioners, CAP-
> PONI, VALORI, BONSI, and VESPUCCI, emerge from
> the Palazzo Pubblico, and occupy the steps of the
> Palace and the Loggia de' Lanzi.   The Crowd fall
> back, lining the square, and leaving a broad space
> for the King and his suite to enter.   Meanwhile
> the following conversations go on.]

FIRST CITIZEN.

Indeed you never saw

A meaner manikin than this French King.

His head is like a pumpkin.

SECOND CITIZEN.

And his nose

As long as a banana, and with legs

Like one laid out.   He scarce bestrides his steed,

With lance in rest I swear he could not couch.

THIRD CITIZEN.

But such a following !   At his heels there march

A hundred of the loveliest youths of France,
Bearing huge cross-bows.   After them, afoot,
Two hundred cavaliers with raiment dipped
In colours of the dawn, and plumes that scorn
The air they sail through.

FIRST CITIZEN.

      Ay, and did you note
The Switzers with cuirasses thrown aside,
As in disdain of who should tilt at them?
The horses have their tail and mane close cropped,
A monstrous sight; in all twelve thousand strong.

SECOND CITIZEN.

And which way are they moving?

FIRST CITIZEN.

       Straight across
Borgo San Frediano, thence along
Fondaccio di San Jacopo, over next
The Ponte Vecchio, grimly entering then
The Canto dei Pazzi.

VOICES.

    Hush! they come!

[By this time the SIGNORY, etc., have taken their places, in state, awaiting the King. CHARLES enters on horseback, lance in rest, attended by STEFANO DI VERS, known as Marshal Beaucaire, MARSHAL BRISSONET, LUDOVICO IL MORO, PHILIPPE DE COMINES, and followed by armed retinue as described above. The People salute the King respectfully, but in silence.]

FIRST CITIZEN.

Look !   That is Il Moro.

SECOND CITIZEN.

                    Black in looks as heart,
The plague of Italy.

FIRST CITIZEN.

                And that's Beaucaire,
A marshal now, but in his youth a groom.

SECOND CITIZEN.

'Twas not for nothing that he learned to ride.

FIRST CITIZEN.

And that's Comines, almost as literate
As any Florentine.   The rest are boors,
Who don't know print from painting.

CAPPONI.

Most Christian King, this city welcomes you,
And is your friend, so you to it extend
Proofs of your friendship.   Passage it gives free
Unto your troops, and will not help withhold
In money and in kind to speed you on.

[He produces a paper.]

But these your terms are too exorbitant.

DE COMINES.

In what do they exceed?

VESPUCCI.

In every clause

We find excess.   We are prepared to give
Twice sixty thousand florins to assist
Your journey forward, not a florin more.

VOICES.

And plenty, too !

DE COMINES.

What else do you except?

VALORI.

The long retention of our fortresses,
Which we demand should be restored to us,
Either within two years, or when the King
His enterprise to Naples hath achieved,
Whichever happens soonest.

DE COMINES.

Well, what more
Would you propose?

BONSI.

That Pisa should receive
No countenance in her rebellion.
The Pisans must submit, and Florence then
Will grant them pardon.

DE COMINES.

Know you these are terms
Grossly in diminution of the bond
Piero de' Medici is with the King
Prepared to ratify?

[At the sound of the name of the MEDICI there is commotion in the Crowd.]

VESPUCCI.

         Piero de' Medici
Is from the Commonwealth of Florence banned.
His pledges bind us not.

DE COMINES.

         But if the King
Prefer his promises to yours, and add
To the conditions you object to, this,
That Florence do take back the Medici ?

VALORI.

Then to the King's most Christian Majesty,
This is the answer.   Friends of the Medici
Are enemies of Florence.   Let him choose.
Which shall it be ?

DE COMINES.

         Sure you forget, the King
Entered your city with his lance in rest ;
And, chalk in hand, his retinue have scored
Your houses as they would.

VALORI.

         Chalk-marks, forsooth,

Are just as easily rubbed out as made ;

And lances laid in rest from rest must vault,

If they mean more than dreaming.

> [DE COMINES looks at the King, who points silently
> to the paper in the hands of PIERO CAPPONI, and
> then at his armed followers.]

DE COMINES.

I am bid

To answer that the terms writ plainly there

Are the King's ultimatum.   If refused,

Well, he will blow his trumpets.

> [CAPPONI tears the paper into fragments, and flings
> them on the ground.]

CAPPONI.

Sound them then !

And we will clang our bells.

> [The People shout, and brandish their arms.   The
> King looks scared.   As soon as silence is restored,
> the King speaks.]

THE KING.

Ah ! Capon ! Capon !   You are a wicked capon !

Then be it as you will !

> [The People cheer tumultuously, and fraternise with
> the French troops ; the SIGNORY, etc., remaining

seated.   Suddenly there is a movement in the
Crowd, and all eyes are turned in the same direction.]

VOICES.

See !   He is coming.

OTHER VOICES.

Whence ?   Where ?   Why ?   Who ?

THE CROWD.

Savonarola !

[Enter SAVONAROLA, attended by FRÀ DOMENICO and
FRÀ SILVESTRO.   The King, who has hitherto
remained covered, lifts his helmet.]

SAVONAROLA.

O most Christian King !
You are the instrument of God that hath
Been sent to mend the woes of Italy,
As I for many a year now have foretold.
Sent are you likewise to reform His Church,
Drunk with iniquity.   But should you fail
In justice or in mercy, should you not
Respect the city of Florence, its honour, its rights,
And, most of all, its liberties, the Lord
Will choose another to execute His work,

And on you then will heavy be His hand,

On you the scourge you should administer.

This in the name of the Lord I say to you :

Stay here you must not, for your sojourn hurts

Both Florence and your march.　You squander
　　　time,

Forgetful of the duty Providence

Upon you hath imposed.　Hearken and obey

The voice of the Servant of God.　If not, the sword

Will snap and splinter in your grasp, and turn

Its jaggëd edge against you.

> [The King makes a sign of assent.　The air rings with
> acclamations.]

SAVONAROLA.

　　　　　　　Thus in peace

Speed you, O Christian King, whom Florence hails

Friend and Protector of her liberties.

> [The King, his suite, and his soldiers, file off the stage.
> When they are gone, SAVONAROLA turns to the
> People.]

SAVONAROLA.

Now hence unto the Duomo, Florentines !

Hence with me, godly citizens, to chant

Te Deum unto Heaven.   The Medici have fled ;

The night is past ; the day of Virtue dawns !

Christ lives, Christ reigns, Christ conquers, Christ is

    King !

    [The People shout *"Evviva Christo !"* Monks, Acolytes,
       and Choristers enter, bearing sacred banners.   A
       Procession is formed, headed by SAVONAROLA,
       who leads the way to the Duomo, chanting the
       Te Deum.   Curtain falls.]

END OF ACT II.

ACT III.

SCENE I.

[A Rectangular Cloister in the Convent of San Marco, its three
sides enclosing a Garden, in the centre of which is a
Sundial.   Five Monks : two of them digging, two
pruning roses, one leaning against a pillar, saying his
rosary.]

FIRST MONK.

How lean and destitute of life he looks !
He were no worse, if preaching.

SECOND MONK.

                              Better, sooth !
It burns him to be silent, and his thoughts,
All egress barred, consume him inwardly.

THIRD MONK.

Besides, he parleys with the world unseen,
And communing with spirits makes the flesh
Tenuous as they themselves are.

FOURTH MONK.

Think you so ?

FIRST MONK.

Look at him well !   He lives in ecstasy,

His body mere commodity of which

The soul makes use, ruthlessly wasting it.

What can a light, when it hath burned too low

But melt the socket ?   So is it with him.

But hush ! he comes.

[Enter SAVONAROLA, followed by FRÀ DOMENICO and
    FRÀ SILVESTRO.   As he does so, the Monk saying
    his rosary genuflects and kisses his hand.]

SAVONAROLA.

Well occupied, my son !

In peace and purity possess your soul.

Pray to Saint Dominick.

[Exit the Monk.   The two that were digging suspend
    their work, and all four draw near to SAVONAROLA.]

SAVONAROLA.

How happy you,

My children, thus to cultivate your flowers !

My garden is a desert, and the voice

Of him that wears Rome's mitre on his head
Forbids that I should work among the weeds.

FRÀ DOMENICO.

Heed him not, Father.   He is ill-informed,
All Florence waits to hear you.

SAVONAROLA.

Then never cease
Importuning the brethren that they pray
To have this Interdict removed.   They should,
Daily, when Matins have been said, recite
The *Alma Redemptoris*, and at close
Of Vespers and of Compline, sing aloud
Ave Regina.   This, with fervent heart,
And Heaven will answer.   Go, and tell them this.

[The four Monks make an obeisance, and depart.]

SAVONAROLA.

Show me again your vision of last night.
It seems alive with apt significance.

FRÀ SILVESTRO.

Over the city of Rome there hung a Cross,
Blacker than night itself, whereon was writ

Crux iræ Dei; a cross that reached to Heaven.
The sky was tattered, and while thunders pealed,
Swords flashed, and flames; and many people died.
Then suddenly the sky grew calm, and I
Was not at Rome, but in Jerusalem,
High above which there rose a Cross of Gold,
That scattered light throughout the Universe,
And on its outstretched arms the inscription bore,
Crux misericordiæ Dei, and all mankind
Thronged to adore it.

SAVONAROLA.

       Heaven and Hell alike
Send their nocturnal embassies, and dreams
From demons as from angels may proceed;
But this seems heavenly.   Prayer alone discerns
Betwixt the upper and the nether world.
Therefore, my son, persist in prayer.   And you,
Dear brother Dominick, still hold in charge
The little ones of Florence, for my sake.
Maintain them innocent.   The buds that burst
Their hull too soon, are rifled by the wind,
Whose rough familiarity had not
Hurt their maturity.

FRÀ DOMENICO.

Ever what you bid,
I strive to do.   On their green hearts I graft
Slips of your teaching.

SAVONAROLA.

Ah ! if I could teach !
[He soliloquises, rather than addresses them ; and they
look on in awe and silence.]

Why do they silence me ?   Yet better peace,
If peace were to be found !   Peace sought too late !
Leaving his home, a youth set out from port,
But when he could no more discern the shore
Whence he had sailed, but only, all around,
The empty cradles of the barren sea,
Bitterly he wept.   O Florence ! that same youth
Who thus bewailed himself, is none but I,
Who in the haven of the cloister found
Freedom and quietude, two things I loved
Above all others, but from these was lured
To toss upon the city's sinful waves,
Spurred by the hope that preaching I might catch
Some souls for God.   Out in the open sea,
O Lord ! Thou hast placed me, and I see no port.

Tempest and tribulation hem me round,

And ever onward urgeth me the wind.

Whither, O God ! hast Thou conducted me ?

Why hast Thou made my name a name of strife,

And cut off my retreat to liberty,

To liberty and peace ?   Once I was free,

But now enslaved to all.   But you, my friends,

Elect of God, for whom both day and night

I struggle in affliction, you, at least,

Have pity upon me !   Give me, give me flowers,

Because with love I languish : flowers of good works,

For these are all I long for, that you be

Pleasing to God, and sanctify your souls.

Now, in this whirlwind, pray that I may have

Repose an instant.

> [He seems overcome, and leans against one of the pillars
> of the Cloister.   Frà Domenico and Frà Silves-
> tro draw nearer to him.   Enter a Lay-brother.]

LAY-BROTHER.

Father, the lady Candida would crave

A conference with you.

SAVONAROLA.

Soul as white as hers

Were not kept waiting at the Gate of Heaven.

Pray her to enter.   Go you now, my sons.

[Exeunt LAY-BROTHER, FRÀ DOMENICO, and FRÀ
SILVESTRO.   Enter CANDIDA.]

SCENE II.

SAVONAROLA.   CANDIDA.

CANDIDA.

Your blessing, Father !

SAVONAROLA.

Daughter, it is yours,
Though you bring blessing with you ; for each door
Through which you pass, invisibly becomes
Door of humility.   What can I do for you ?

CANDIDA.

There is a maiden nestled in my heart,
And whose uncounted tenderness is spent
On one who, though of worthy elements,
Is with the mundane enemies allied
Of you and Florence.

SAVONAROLA.

Doth that come between
Him and her love?

CANDIDA.

No! She is like the moon,
That never turns but one face to the earth,
Being so true a satellite.

SAVONAROLA.

And you
The centre of his orbit fain would shift,
Hers keeping fixed?

CANDIDA.

That, Father, is my prayer,
Which you alone can grant!   Sometimes I fear
That passionate love hath twisted them awry,
Like trees that help each other out of shape,
And lose their heavenly perpendicular
By too close interlocking of their boughs.
Yet separate them not; but only lift
Their love more heavenward!

SAVONAROLA.

How may that be done,

Not done already?   See how many souls
Are sliding to perdition, whom my hand
Might yet pluck back !   Yes, I must preach, I must,
Though thousand Borgias bid me to be mute.
Daughter, I may not preach, so cannot save.
There is an interdict upon my tongue.
Yet, if I preach, bring this revolted soul
Unto the Duomo !

CANDIDA.

May that· quickly be,
Lest he grow hardened in rebellion.
I thank you, Father.

> [She turns to go.]

SAVONAROLA.

Tell me, my child, how fares
Valori's suit with your reluctant heart ?

CANDIDA.

I willingly had been the bride of Heaven,
Had you not banned that nuptial; wherefore, now,
I linger in perplexity, my will
Petitioned by two hearts, I know not why,
Being of each unworthy.

SAVONAROLA.

     Doubt not, child,
Which is the worthier.   Tornabuoni plots
Against the liberties of Florence, whilst
Valori still upholds them.

CANDIDA.

    These are things
Beyond my ken; though, Father, it hath seemed
To my scant vision that a valiant arm,
Committed to the State, needs all its nerve
For that tough task, and I should hamper it
With my small needs and weak defencelessness.

SAVONAROLA.

Weakness like yours may double a man's strength;
And so, my child, discourage him no more.
Men, when they love, see angels in a dream,
As Jacob did.   Be you the stair whereby
Valori's earthlier aspirations may
Communicate with Heaven.

CANDIDA.

      I were content,
Could I to such celestial use be put,

To learn the purport of this earthly love,
Which seems the native language of mankind,
Though I was born a mute.

SAVONAROLA.

'Tis not amiss,
Where such a tongue is spoken, maidens should
Be dumb, provided that they are not deaf.
So when Valori whispers you, give ear
Even to accents of the earthliest sound,
And from the heights of Heaven reply to him.

[Enter a LAY-BROTHER.]

LAY-BROTHER.

Signor Valori, Father, awaits without.

SAVONAROLA.

Admit him.

[Exit LAY-BROTHER.]

CANDIDA.

But not—not—

[SAVONAROLA opens a side-door in the garden-wall.]

SAVONAROLA.

Dear child ! pass through

Into the outer world, and take with you

The cloister of your purity.

    [Exit CANDIDA.   Enter VALORI from interior of the
      Convent.]

SCENE III.

SAVONAROLA.   VALORI.

SAVONAROLA.

           You bring

Grave news, Valori.

VALORI.

           Graver never brought.

You know how lightly still the French King holds

His promises to Florence.   Not his word,

Sworn in the Duomo on the Gospels, nor

Your threats and prophecies have kept him leal.

For fourteen thousand florins hath he sold

Their freedom to the Pisans, and for ten

All the artillery collected there.

Genoa for twenty thousand florins gets

Sarzana, and for thirty Lucca holds

Pietrasanta.

SAVONAROLA.

    Facts, though grave, not new.
Have you none younger?

VALORI.

    Since Capponi died,
Mortally stricken at Soiana, none
Of all our Captains have into our camp
Fortune seduced; and I am loath to turn
My back upon the city, wherein plot
Bigi, Arrabbiati, all the foes
Of the Grand Council and free government,
Once by your voice established, but now left
To me to uphold.   The Ottimati, now
The Medici no longer govern, men
Like Bonsi and Vespucci, help no more,
But rather thwart.

SAVONAROLA.

    The Pope hath silenced me.
How can I speak?

VALORI.

    The League astutely formed
By Ludovico Il Moro 'twixt himself,

The Pope, and Venice, to our detriment,
Soon as King Charles was back in France, enticed
The Emperor Maximilian o'er the Alps.
He, well received in Pisa, now blockades
The port of Leghorn, with the aid of ships
Procured from Venice.

SAVONAROLA.

           Do you think that news
So sharp and pointed hath not pierced these walls?
But you talk politics of earth, that here
Are close on sacrilege.   What have I to do
With your affairs of State?   A thousand times
I have protested, and I still protest,
That such is not my office.   If I helped
To heal your discords, and establish laws
That shelter liberty and virtue, know,
I did it for God's glory, not for man.
What did men say?   This Friar thirsts for power,
For gold, and for the Cardinal's red robe.
O Lord! that searchest hearts, the robe I want
Is the red robe of martyrdom alone,
Thou givest to thy Saints!   O give it me quick,
And end my tribulations!

VALORI (*aside*).

                    He is rapt
In ecstasy, his mind above the ground.
How shall I draw him back ?   But, Prior, see,
The currents of the upper and lower air
Are ofttimes contrary ; yet 'tis the last
Which sway the motion of the things that have
Their roothold in the earth.   The nearest thought
To every heart in Florence, as you know,
Is to recover Pisa.

SAVONAROLA.

                    And to mine,
The nearest, to recover souls to God.
You would see Florence great, and so would I,
But great in goodness.   You mistake my end,
You with the rest.

VALORI.

                    If once the people think
Charles of Anjou will play us ever false,
Whereas the League, if joined, would give us back
Pisa, with all the Tuscan fortresses,
The very Piagnoni will demand
That profitable compact.   Charles our foe,

Your prophecies all falsified, the base
Of your celestial menaces collapsed,
Where then would be your hold upon their hearts?
Already they are clamouring for a sign
To prove that you misled them not, when first
You in the pulpit welcomed the French King
As the New Cyrus and the Scourge of God.

SAVONAROLA.

And such he was, and such will he return,
If they repent not.   Did I not foretell
His speedy punishment if he forbore
To renovate God's Church?   And now what news?
Is not his eldest son, the Dauphin, dead?
What sign do they want?   If needed, it will come.
But Thine, O Lord, the moment, Thine the hour,
Not theirs to ask for, and not mine to grant.

VALORI.

Still rambling 'mong the clouds.   But hear you more!
Lamberto dell' Antella, venturing back
Without our leave to Tuscan territory,
Hath been arrested, and, by papers found
Upon his person, evidence provides

Of a conspiracy to reinstate
Piero de' Medici.

SAVONAROLA.

And with whose help?

VALORI.

The help of more than I can stay to count;
But chief among the treasonable band
Del Nero, Niccolò Ridolfi, with
Lorenzo Tornabuoni, Pucci, Cambi,
Men all of note.

SAVONAROLA.

So to be noted well.
The Medici must not return.

VALORI.

Then you must stir
The people with your voice, not leave to me
Sole weight of government.　Piero once back,
Infested would again the city be
With luxury and lust; their songs obscene
And impure revelries once more usurp
The streets of Florence.

SAVONAROLA.

That may never be.
Christ bids me preach ; no Pope shall silence me.
Go tell the people I exhort them bear
From out its shrine the sacred effigy
Of the Madonna dell' Impruneta round
The city walls, and wait for farther news.
Then, if our enemies be routed not,
I straight towards Pisa, crucifix in hand,
Will march, to raise the siege.

VALORI.

But you will preach ?

SAVONAROLA.

God, Who knows all things, knows if I shall preach ;
Press me no more.   My message bear to them,
And see, Valori, treat you leniently
Lorenzo Tornabuoni.

VALORI.

Wherefore him ?

SAVONAROLA.

Because he is young and gallant.

VALORI.

                            With more years
And more seductive graces to conspire
Against the Commonwealth.   Del Nero's craft,
With Tornabuoni's vigour yoked, would make
The unlikeliest plots succeed.   Together they
Have striven to rise ; together let them fall !

[Enter FRÀ DOMENICO and FRÀ SILVESTRO, and a
LAY-BROTHER.]

FRÀ DOMENICO.

Frà Mariano, the Franciscan monk,
The slimiest of your enemies, demands
Admission to the Convent.

SAVONAROLA.

Tell him to enter.   Frà Silvestro, see
All the community be present here,
To hear his words.

[Exeunt LAY-BROTHER and FRÀ SILVESTRO.]

VALORI.

                    Prior, I take my leave.
But wanting not in reverence, I adjure
You heed.my point.

SAVONAROLA.

Guard well the Commonwealth.

[Exit VALORI.]

SCENE IV.

SAVONAROLA.   FRÀ DOMENICO.

FRÀ DOMENICO.

The cunning of this sly Franciscan bodes
No blessing to the Convent.   He hath ne'er
Forgiven your diversion of the ears
Of Florence from his preaching.

SAVONAROLA.

Let him come,
Bring he or ban or blessing to our cells.
Christ lives, Christ reigns.

[Enter from the Convent FRÀ MARIANO DA GENEZ-
ZANO, with Ecclesiastical Attendants.   At the same
time the Monks of San Marco pour into the
cloister.]

FRÀ MARIANO.

I bear with me the Brief

In every church in Florence to be read,
Of Excommunication launched against
Savonarola, Frà Girolamo,
Who calls himself the Prior of Saint Mark.

[He reads.]

" This Frà Girolamo, obeying not
Our apostolic admonition, sent
Time after time, that he repair to Rome,
And duly make submission at our feet ;
And equally neglecting our decree,
Which in the Congregation newly formed
Of Rome and Tuscany hath henceforth merged
The Convent of Saint Mark, he claims to rule,
Is hereby excommunicate, and must
By all as such be held, who well are warned,
That, holding converse or communion
With this same Frà Girolamo, they will
Themselves incur an equal penalty."

SAVONAROLA.

Have you your mission executed ?

FRÀ MARIANO.

Yes.

M

SAVONAROLA.

Then leave me with my brethren.   I can lend
No further welcome here.

[Exeunt FRÀ MARIANO and his Attendants.]

SAVONAROLA.

                    My sons, you have heard ;
And hearing, now decide.   Are you content
In this new Congregation to be merged ?

FRÀ DOMENICO.

Never ; save, Father, you abandon us.
Is not that so ?

MONKS.

It is !   It is !

SAVONAROLA.

                    Remember,
Once merged in it your rule were lighter far
Than that I place upon you.   You would have
Less prayer and fewer fasts, more sleep, more taste
Of carnal comfort.

FRÀ SILVESTRO.

But we wish them not.

MONKS.

Nor we.

OTHER MONKS.

Nor we !

SAVONAROLA.

Beware how you decide.
This road may lead to martyrdom.   The Keys
Of Peter now are grasped by one who gained,
Through means notoriously simoniacal,
The Papal Chair.   Christ's Vicar he is not,
And there must be a Council of the Church
To test his claims.   But meanwhile he will plot
With our sworn enemies in Florence here
To baffle this intent.   Are you prepared
To follow me, if need be, to the stake,
To purify the Church of God, and keep
Christ as the King of Florence?

MONKS.

Yes, all, all, all.

SAVONAROLA.

Then shall I preach again,

Though when, I know not; but I cannot live,
Live and not preach.

> [The Monks make way for Savonarola, who enters
> the Chapel of the Convent alone.]

SCENE V.

> [A Street in Florence.   Enter (right) Candida   and
> Letizia.]

LETIZIA.

He bade me meet him here.

CANDIDA.

We are too soon.

LETIZIA.

Love ne'er was late; and neither, look, is he.
See where he comes, and, with him, happiness.

> [Enter Bettuccio (left).]

LETIZIA.

Sweet, here is one who a request would make

BETTUCCIO.

One unto whom request was ne'er refused
By man, I warrant.

CANDIDA.

Then, 'tis granted me ?

BETTUCCIO.

Before 'tis uttered.

CANDIDA.

'Tis a simple wish ;
That you Letizia will accompany,
When next discourses Frà Girolamo
Within the Duomo.

BETTUCCIO.

Anywhere with her.
Will you conduct us ?

CANDIDA.

Never have I missed
One lesson through his sacred lips distilled.
It is a compact.

BETTUCCIO.

One I will not break.

But, lady, I this moment heard strange news,

That may concern you.   Papers have been found

That implicate five leading citizens

In a conspiracy to reinstate

The Medici in Florence ; 'mong the five,

Lorenzo Tornabuoni.

CANDIDA.

Ever rash

In snatching at a branch he cannot reach !

Think you he stands in danger ?

BETTUCCIO.

In so much,

That, were I he, Florence should see my heels

Before it heard the Angelus.

CANDIDA.

Then go,

Apprise him quick ! Letizia ! let us haste

On the same errand.   Peril pleads for him

Better than he himself.   You to his house,

While I will aid him more circuitously.

[Exeunt CANDIDA and LETIZIA (right).   BETTUCCIO
        crosses the stage to leave (left).   As he does so,
        enter GROSSO'S Wife.   He runs against her.]

BETTUCCIO.

Where go you thus in haste ?

ANITA.

                                    I go to join
The great Procession Frà Girolamo
Ordains to rescue Pisa.

BETTUCCIO.

                                    With the aid
Of statues and old women !   Pretty help !
Swords and young limbs were likelier.

ANITA.

                                Won't you come ?

BETTUCCIO.

No, take your husband.

ANITA.

                            Taking 's easy said.
But he's so took with statues of his own,
And not a stitch upon them !

BETTUCCIO.

Fare you well !

Go, rescue Pisa.

[Exit (right).   Enter People of all ages (left).]

FIRST CITIZEN.

Come along ! this way !

The statue is got ready.

SECOND CITIZEN.

It will pass

Through the main streets with hymns and litanies.

ANITA.

Yes ; and with candles burning.

[They pass across the stage, ANITA with them, and so
    exeunt (right). As the last of them file away, enter
    (left) DEL NERO, RIDOLFI, and TORNABUONI.]

SCENE VI.

RIDOLFI. DEL NERO. TORNABUONI.

RIDOLFI.

> See the last device
Of this religious mountebank to dupe
The trivial crowd.

DEL NERO.

> A clever trick withal,
Suggested by Valori for his ends.
For superstitious piety, like wine,
Mounts to the brain and heats it fervently.

TORNABUONI.

Pity that Piero neither drinks nor prays,
And so lacks courage for each enterprise.
Petrucci of Siena lent him aid
Beyond all hope; and thirteen hundred men
Bartolommeo d' Alviano raised,
Were ample for the deed.

RIDOLFI.

> Besides, the gate

Of San Piero Gattolini stood
Open, to let him through.

DEL NERO.

        What avails force
To them that hesitate ?   Wide-open gates
But point the way for cowards to contempt.
Let us forget him.

RIDOLFI.

        That, perchance, were wise
If you were Gonfaloniere still ;
But, with a hostile Signory, our plans
May, though abortive, from the ground be dug.

DEL NERO.

Then do not contemplate their grave, lest thus
You draw attention from our enemies.
Now surely it were safer for us all,
Like a wise wind that lays itself to sleep
When once it learns its fierce fatuity,
To keep a neutral calm.

TORNABUONI.

        Counsel, if safe,
Not very soaring.

DEL NERO.

                    Have you never marked,
In cloudy weather, that the birds fly low?
Disdain not their instruction; for it is
The privilege of reason to grow wise
By noting tricks of instinct.   Fare you well!

RIDOLFI.
                    [Taking DEL NERO's arm.]
I have an errand leading me your way.
                              [To TORNABUONI.]
Heed what he says, and in this stumbling world
Learn, boy, to walk a thought more warily.
                              [Exeunt (left).]

TORNABUONI.

When blood grows cold by chilling of old age,
Men call it wisdom.   Then how wise were death,
'Neath whose convincing frost the forward stream
Of slackening impulse stagnates and congeals.
But life means youth, youth signifies resolve,
And 'twixt resolve and action should intrude
No interval more long than takes to lift
The blade that is to fall!

          [He crosses the stage (right).   Enter CANDIDA in haste
            (right).]

CANDIDA.

O fly, sir ! fly !

TORNABUONI.

Fly ?   Anywhere with you !   Where shall it be ?

CANDIDA.

Waste not the precious seconds in retort.
Your liberty, perchance your life, exists
On prompt escape.

TORNABUONI.

Why, you are out of breath !
How did you lose it ?

CANDIDA.

O, in seeking you.

TORNABUONI.

Whom hitherto, alas ! you always fled.

CANDIDA.

You never were in danger ; now you are ;
O, be advised, and fly !

TORNABUONI.

　　　　　While you remain !
How small you measure me ! Though you refuse
To admit me to the region of your breath,
Something it is to draw the selfsame air
That you inhale, and fancy I absorb
Into my lungs the zephyrs that have coursed
Through your sweet veins.

CANDIDA.

　　　　　O, this but madness is.

TORNABUONI.

Madness that you would reckon sanity,
Did you but share it.   See ! these senseless stones
Are to me by your footsteps vivified.
Though each street corner hid a dagger's point,
I should select a danger where you dwelt,
Than dull security on any ground
That was by you untrodden.

CANDIDA.

　　　　　O, you throw
Your life away !

TORNABUONI.

What is my life to you?
To you being nought, it nothing is to me.

CANDIDA.

It is so much to me, I fain would save it.

TORNABUONI.

Then save it by the only way that serves,
For all else kills.   Life severed from your love
Is to me death made sensitive, a corpse
Interred before pulsation be extinct.
You bury me alive; the hands you dread
Would, kindlier, kill outright.

CANDIDA.

What can I more?
My life is mine to give, and I would give it
To save you, sir; but, for my love——

TORNABUONI.

It is
Not yours to give, then to another given.

CANDIDA.

I said not so.

TORNABUONI.

Need none is there to say.
Love, e'en in madness, reasons not amiss.
Farewell, and let me settle with my foes.

CANDIDA.

O, I beseech you !

   [Enter armed OFFICERS of the SIGNORY.]

OFFICER.

Sir, the Signory
Have your arrest decreed, and we are here
To execute their order, under which
Signors Del Nero and Ridolfi lie
Already locked in durance.

TORNABUONI.

     Fare you well !
The road to death, if now 'tis to be walked,
Will by your obduracy smooth be made,
O lovely executioner !

  [Exit (left) with Officers. He turns to gaze at CANDIDA,
    who covers her face with her hands. Meanwhile
    LETIZIA has entered (right). She approaches
    CANDIDA.]

CANDIDA.

Too late ! Too late ! Lead me away : I would
Be left alone a little.

[Exit CANDIDA (right), supported by LETIZIA.]

SCENE VII.

[The sound of singing is heard, and a Procession, following the Statue of the Madonna dell' Impruneta
enters (left), and passes round the stage. When
it has done so, enter (right) MARCUCCIO SAL-
VIATI ; behind him, COMPAGNACCI and ARRAB-
BIATTI, laughing, and shrugging their shoulders
scornfully.]

SALVIATI.

Joyous news !

A messenger on horseback passed but now
Through Porta San Frediano, spurring on
Unto the Signory.   His tidings are,
Ships from Marseilles, despatched by the French King,
Bearing relief for Leghorn, have been borne
Straight into port, despite the enemy,
By a Libeccio wind, which timely rose,
And Leghorn, crammed with victuals, is secure
Against all hazards.

FIRST PIAGNONE.

Who will argue now
Savonarola cannot prophesy?

SECOND PIAGNONE.

And who will say he does not help the State?

FIRST ARRABBIATO.

You have not got back Pisa.

FIRST PIAGNONE.

But we will.

SECOND ARRABBIATO.

From whom?　From Charles or Maximilian?
The Pisans flung the statue of the King
Into the river when the Emperor came.

SALVIATI.

Whither his statue likewise will be thrown,
Save he go homewards.　Frà Girolamo
Hath prophesied this would-be King of Rome
Will quick recross the Alps.

FIRST ARRABBIATO.

What if he do?

That will not upon Pisa's stubborn neck

Reset the foot of Florence, or compel

Its population, as of old, to kiss

The quarters of 'Marzocco!'

SECOND ARRABBIATO.

That's the point.

We're for the League, if it will give us back

The fortresses and Pisa.

CROWD.

Down with the League!

And long live Savonarola!

[The Procession forms afresh, and exit (left), followed
by the COMPAGNACCI and ARRABBIATI, scoffing.
Enter (right) CANDIDA and LETIZIA.]

LETIZIA.

Shall we unto the Convent?

CANDIDA.

No! 'twere wise

To seek a worldlier counsellor; one of late

I have too much avoided.

LETIZIA.

　　　　　　　　　　　　　　　　Shall I guess
Your lay auxiliary ?

CANDIDA.

You surmise his name.

LETIZIA.

He will grant more than ever you can ask ;
For love, in giving, is a prodigal.

CANDIDA.

'Tis not for love that I would have him give,
Robbing his virtue, granting it reward.'
He for unhiring mercy's sake must spare
Lorenzo Tornabuoni.   It may be
That we have saved Bettuccio's soul this day.
A body is in peril ; let us save
That also.   Then,—well, we will weep and pray.

　　　　　　　　　　　　　　　　[Exeunt (left).]

SCENE VIII.

[Enter (right) a number of young boys dressed like angels,
and carrying large open baskets.]

FIRST CHILD.

Good folks! good folks!   Bring out your Vanities!
We are collecting them for Carnival.

SECOND CHILD.

Bring out your Vanities, that they may burn,
Pictures, and books, and love-songs, naughty tales,
And poems, worst of all.

THIRD CHILD.

                    Quick, bring them out,
That we may make a bonfire of the leaves,
And dance around their ashes.

FIRST CHILD.

                    Vanities!
Who has more Vanities?

[Men and women come out of the houses, bearing books,
pictures, and other objects, and give them to the
children.]

FIRST CITIZEN.

A wicked book.
'Tis the *Decamerone*, written by
Boccaccio of Certaldo.   Better burnt!
Twice I have read it through, and I were fain
My wife did not.

SECOND CITIZEN.

A wise precaution, friend.
I have two copies, and perhaps 'twere well
That one should burn.   The other will I keep,
To make quite sure its fellow did deserve
Not to survive.

FIRST CHILD.

Vanities! Vanities!
Fetch out your Vanities!

THIRD CITIZEN.

Here!   Take you this:
The *Enchiridion*, translated by
Poliziano in the Latin tongue.
I cannot read it; but my confessor
Declares 'tis full of wickedness.

FOURTH CITIZEN.

                              Here's a prize :

Antonio Panhormita's famous work,

Hermaphroditus, and along with it,

Poggio's *Facetiæ ;* rather past a joke.

You're welcome to 't.

                    [Flings it into the basket of one of the children.]

FIFTH CITIZEN.

                        Who sent you here to cry

Your wares beneath our windows all day long ?

SECOND CHILD.

Savonarola sends us, sir, to beg,

And not to buy ; to beg the Devil's works,

And so give alms to Christ.

THIRD CHILD.

                              And we are trained

By Frà Domenico of Pescia,

Who loves the Prior of Saint Mark almost

As Frà Girolamo loves Christ Himself.

ALL THE CHILDREN.

Vanities !   Vanities !   Ransack your Vanities !

SIXTH CITIZEN.

All Pico's Works, and all Politian's.
They are too learned for me; but I daresay
They are as thick with wrong as a dark wood
With thieves and ghosts.

SEVENTH CITIZEN.

         Now mark you, never say
I made no sacrifice.   I paid for these
Five florins on the nail.   See, they contain
Luigi Pulci's poems; first there comes
Morgante Maggiore; next—but well,
I will not say what next; but burn them all.
What have you there?

    [To another Citizen, who brings out a bundle of books.
      All crowd round him.]

EIGHTH CITIZEN.

" *Selve d'Amore,*" by Lorenzo's self.
" *Canzoni a ballo.*"

SEVENTH CITIZEN.

        Why, you never mean
To give up those?   They are such merry lays,

The dumb would sing them, and the lame would dance,
Hearing their cadence.

       [A book falls to the ground.   The sixth Citizen picks it
       up.]

SIXTH CITIZEN.

              What have we got here?
Canti Carnascialeschi!   O, I say,
These must not be destroyed.   Full half of them
Are great Lorenzo's, written in his prime.
They sing themselves, as rippling waters do,
And foot it as they sing.   I mind me well
Treading a jocund round when I was young
To more than one of these.   Ha! Here it is!
Ben venga Maggio.
            [Shuts the book, and hands it back.]
           Ah! May comes no more
To one whose leaves are half upon the ground,
One half upon the branches, soon to fall!

CHILDREN.

Vanities! Vanities! Any more Vanities?
Bring them and pile them up, that we may search
Their wickedness with fire.

[The boys pass across the stage and exeunt (left). At
the same time enter (right) young girls, clad in
white, and, like the boys, carrying open crates and
baskets.]

FIRST GIRL.

Vanities ! Vanities ! Bring out your Vanities !
Rouge-pots and scented girdles, spices, gums,
Snares of the Evil One !

SECOND GIRL.

Ferret them out,
Unguents and patches, tresses false, and tricks
Of meretricious beauty, specious dyes,
Henna, vermilion, all of them Vanities.
Give them all up !

[Women come out of the houses, and put into the
baskets pots, boxes, and caskets.]

THIRD GIRL.

Where are your books of dreams,
Your amorous astrology, your cards
Of wicked conjuring, your secret store
Of light love-ditties, all of them Vanities !

[Grosso's Wife emerges from a house, carrying books.]

ANITA.

Here they are, girls !   I want no more of them ;
Love-ditties by the score.   When I was young,
My Grosso used to flute them all night long
Under my casement, while I listening sate
Behind the lattice, and conceived no harm.
They sounded very sweet.   But I must own,
Now I am riper, when I hear them trilled
To budding maids at midnight, that they sound
Wrong, very wrong.

FIRST GIRL.

Vanities ! Vanities !
Give up your curls, your counterfeits, your lures,
Love-philtres, and your Lydian potions mixed
By alchemists of Hell !

[All the time women keep bringing out objects which
they deposit in the baskets.]

ANITA.

Wait just a bit,
And I will fetch you such a hecatomb,
It ought to buy me Heaven.

[Re-enters the house from which she came.]

SECOND GIRL.

                Give up your drugs,
Intoxicating perfumes, subtle scents,
That lull the soul to slumber and arouse
The sleeping senses in their swinish sty,
And make them nose for garbage. Give them all up:
Lascivious fripperies, corsets, and the bait
Of perforated sandals!

      [ANITA returns, carrying long rolls of paper.]

ANITA.

        Here they are!
To whom shall I entrust them?

      [A Girl holds out her hand for them.]

ANITA.

           Mind you, child,
You must not look at them, not even peep;
They are so shocking.

   [She unrolls one of them, and hurriedly rolls it up again,
      putting her hand before her eyes.]

ANITA.

      Oh! too terrible!
Shameless as the originals, and nude

E'en as at birth or death !   Take special care
Not one of them escapes the virtuous flames.
How could he sketch such things ?   But having caused
Those to be shrivelled, surely I may keep
One little box of ointments ?   Is it wrong
To put spring roses upon autumn cheeks,
To keep a husband faithful ?

FIRST GIRL.

               Vanities !
Have all your Vanities been yielded up ?
If not, bring out, bring out, more Vanities,
Till none be left.

ANITA.

            I tell you what I'll do :—
Give them the robe I bought for Carnival
The year Lorenzo died.   'T has ne'er been worn,
Nor will be now, too gorgeous for the times.
I'll fetch it straight.

    [She turns to go for it, then halts, and hesitates.]

ANITA.

        No ! stay ! I'll have it dyed.
               [Exit into her house.]

ALL THE GIRLS.

Vanities ! Vanities ! Bring out your Vanities !

All of your Vanities bring out to burn.

> [As they say this they pass away from the stage, some
> right, some left.   The scene rises, and changes to
> the Piazza of the Signoria.]

SCENE IX.

PIAZZA OF THE SIGNORIA.

[In the middle of the Piazza rises a pyramidal octangular scaffolding, filled with faggots, and containing fifteen tiers of shelves
for the articles that are to be burnt, many of which are
already placed there.   The boys that have been collecting
objects for the bonfire enter (left), and the young girls enter
(right).   Other people, among them BETTUCCIO, come upon
the stage, bearing in their hands pictures, books, and some
of them statues, and these they lay upon the pyramidal
scaffolding.   FRÀ DOMENICO and three other MONKS of
San Marco superintend the operation.   BONSI and VES-
PUCCI stand apart, and look on.]

FIRST PIAGNONE.

See ! There's Bettuccio carrying his load.

He used to howl with the wolves.

SECOND PIAGNONE.

And now he bleats

Like any lamb that's ready to be shorn.
Savonarola has converted him.

THIRD PIAGNONE.

And many another.   What have you got here?

BETTUCCIO.

Only some worthless verses and designs,
That in the heyday of my fatuous joy
I used to fancy precious.

FIRST PIAGNONE.

     Are they your own?

BETTUCCIO.

Only our vices are our own, good friend,
And these, to cure ; the rest belong to Heaven.
This is my contribution.

SECOND PIAGNONE.

     Verily,
Our Frà Girolamo works miracles.
Never before did poet burn his verse
At bidding of another.

THIRD PIAGNONE.

Did you hear,
Bartolommeo Baccio gives to the flames
His drawings from the nude?

BETTUCCIO.

Yes, and what's more—
Lorenzo Credi swells the holocaust
With his lewd sketches.

BONSI.

I have heard it said,
When beasts go mad, they hasten to devour
Their litter, the most comely offspring first.
These Whimperers do the same.   I would have given
A thousand crowns for some of Baccio's work.

VESPUCCI.

Heed not : the fair originals remain,
And are in every season reproduced
By love, who casts them in a gracious mould.
Thus Nature, never foiled in her designs,
And inly smiling at the sour excess
Of these ephemeral fanatics, will prompt

Some other artist to repair the loss.
Come, let us leave them.

BONSI.

>   Rather let us watch

Their austere antics.

> [They stand aside, and look on, while men, women,
> boys, girls, and monks, join hands, and make a
> circle round the pyramid, which, as they begin to
> dance round it, is set fire to.]

FRÀ DOMENICO.

>   Now then to begin.

Who has the torch?

SECOND PIAGNONE.

>   'Tis here.

FRÀ DOMENICO.

>   Then in with it.

Hark how the faggots crackle!   It has caught.
Who gives the air?

THIRD PIAGNONE.

>   Why, all of us must sing.

'Tis " *Una donna d' amor fino.*"

SEVERAL VOICES.

Oh!

FRÀ DOMENICO.

Nay, be not shocked; the air is innocent,
Weaned from the rhymes that suckled it.　It was
A song of sin; but if we it baptize
With holy words, it straightway will become
A canticle of grace.

BONSI.

There he is right.
Have you observed it is the privilege
Of unexplicit harmony to foil
Art's meretricious purposes till joined
With an unworthy consort, and, divorced
From the light tie of language, to resume
Its abstract purity?

VESPUCCI.

I have noted it.
But I was rather thinking, give me leave,
That 'tis the common foible of mankind
Ever to sing new words to the old tune.
That changeth not.　Hark! they are singing it now!

[The circle being complete, and their hands joined, the
company dance round the burning Vanities, singing,
as they do so, the following hymn.]

I

No greater honour in life than this,

No richer guerdon, no deeper bliss,

Ever can mortal have or had,

Than for love of Christ to go stark mad:

　　Mad, mad, utterly mad,

　　　Wittingly, cheerfully, happily mad!

II.

They whom the world think sound and sane

Run after pleasure and fly from pain

We court penury, weeping, woe,

The poor man's curse and the rich man's blow

　　Because we are mad, stark staring mad,

　　　For the love of Christ perversely mad!

[Fresh people pour in; one of them bearing aloft on a
pole the portrait of a Jew.]

FIRST PIAGNONE.

What may this be ?

NEW COMER.

It is the effigy

Of a rich Hebrew who would fain have bought
For twenty thousand florins in a lump
These Vanities we burn.

SECOND NEW COMER.

                So we thought
That we would burn him too, at least so far
As goes combustion in these clement days.

CROWD.

Evivva Cristo ! Put him on the pile.

    [The portrait of the Jew is hoisted up, and surmounts
        the burning pyramid of Vanities.   Then the people
        dance and sing again.]

Who wants a medicine for his soul?

Here is the recipe ! Bring the bowl.

Throw in five ounces of Hope, and six

Of unquestioning Faith ; then duly mix.

Pour in a pound of Love, and three

Of the finest syrup of Charity.

Humility's quintessential oil

Put in the last, and leave to boil.

   And this will make you perfectly mad ;

      Mad, mad, mad, mad ;

    For the love of Christ divinely mad !

[By this time the fire begins to burn low, all the Vanities
    being consumed. . The dancers are out of breath,
    halt, and disjoin hands.]

FIRST PIAGNONE.

I' faith, how quickly have the flames devoured
Their wicked forage.

A MONK.

                Leave them alone ; they know
There is much virtue in a good hot fire.

BONSI.

Then there must be much virtue, friend, in Hell.
Is that sound doctrine ?   Better have a care
Lest you be burnt yourself.

FRÀ DOMENICO.

                The virtuous flames
He meant are rather those of Purgatory.

VESPUCCI.

Then all the ashes of the things you have burnt
In time will go to Heaven ?   That's heresy,
Bad as the first.

FRÀ DOMENICO.

Your logic may be good,
But dialectics never saved a soul.

SECOND PIAGNONE.

What shall we do with the ashes?

THIRD PIAGNONE.

                                    Wheel them on,
And drown them in the Arno.

VOICES.

                        Off we go!

[They trundle the pyramid off the stage, some pulling,
    some pushing, others pressing round it.   Exeunt
    gradually (right).]

BONSI.

See how they press the blameless elements
Into their bitter service!   Heaven forfend
We have not other burnings worse than this,
Which is the obverse side of levity.
None but our carnal Florence could invent
So strange a carnival.

VESPUCCI.

I sometimes think
It needs the froward fluctuating air,
Between the hills and valleys buffeted,
Of this fair city, to produce such shifts
Of keen emotion.

BONSI.

Think you this will pass?

VESPUCCI.

You know the Florentines.   They ever were
The substance out of which, when stars consent,
You get your poets, painters, and such like,
Quick, lissom, volatile, the very wood
Wherefrom to make a crowd of Mercuries.
Look how they run!   The herald of the Gods
Could skip no faster.

BONSI.

But this earnest monk,
Savonarola, seems to hold them fast,
And sets them at the point of seriousness.

VESPUCCI.

Unto that quarter never were they fixed.

If they affect it now, 'tis from the mood
That sets the west wind backing to the north
When April is with zephyrs surfeited
And looks behind for March, though May's afront,
And will be welcomed wantonly.

> [Enter GROSSO (left), precipitately.]

GROSSO.

> Good sirs !

Can you direct me where our madcap saints
Are burning all the relics of the gods
Who were reputed to have died in Greece,
But in this age have come to life again,
The gods of beauty, joy, and spaciousness ?
I thought 'twas here.

BONSI.

> And so it was.   But now

The bonfire of their bigotry is spent,
And Arno holds its ashes.

GROSSO.

> Say not so !

O, you but mock me ! There is time to save
What unto me is dearer than my life,
My past, my future !

VESPUCCI.

But he mocks you not.
Your dearest, then, is gone.   What may it be ?

GROSSO.

O, then the gods are dead who would not stretch
A helping hand to shield their effigies !
Gone ! burnt to smoke ! parched cinders in the dust,
That I let suck my life-blood ! dreamed at night,
To do by day, the cunning of my hand
Following my bent as speech obeys the brain,
All shrivelled into ashes !   O sirs !   I,
Who never prated of myself before,
Am now so probed and pestered to the quick,
That the whole universe seems filled with *Me*,
And we are wronged together !

BONSI.

He doth bewail his labours late consumed
In the quick oven of that foolish fire.

VESPUCCI.

A touching sight !   The children of their thought
Are dearer to these men than carnal sons,

Since that they get them and they bear them too.

Such generation and conception are

Lodged in the single organ of the brain.

A fantasy of nature, Genius is

A vigorous hermaphrodite that teems.

By brooding on itself, nor ever needs

Marriage with other minds.

BONSI.

　　　　　　He seems distraught

Think you he meditates to take the road

Whither his fancies have preceded him?

Speak him a word of comfort.

VESPUCCI.

[Approaching to Grosso, who has seated himself on a
marble bench, his face buried in his hands.]

　　　　　　Worthy friend,

Are you not too determined in despair?

How know you that your pretty things were thrust

Into those flames fanatical?

GROSSO.

　　　　　　[Starting up.]

　　　　How do I know it!

I have a wife, the halver of my bed,

My shadow, substance, flesh of very flesh,
Bone of my bone, a chain that gnaws into them,
A dead negation not to be denied,
A dearer self, that holds me, O so cheap!
That what there is of me that is not her,
She reckons just as nought!   A wife! a wife!
A murderess throttling all my babes at once,
Because she neither bore nor suckled them!
All my unfinished studies! naked, yes!
Naked as is the sky, as is the spring,
As Eve before the fancied fall, as Heaven,
Radiant, unraimented!   Gone! all of them gone,
And my poor meaning with them!

BONSI.

                     But, good friend!
Your cunning may this gaping loss replace.
As many maiden models walk the earth
As sleep within its bosom, and no boon
Welcomer than this their modesty could wish,
That you should lift their loveliness to Heaven,
And fix them into immortality.

GROSSO.

Can you rewind the ticking of the brain

That hath run down its hour ?   Why, look at me !
Alas ! my hairs are straggling gossamer,
And, like the seeded dandelion, good
Only to tell the time by !

VESPUCCI.

You are hale
To common seeming, and might procreate still
A lusty brood of fancies.

GROSSO.

Out on you,
If you have been a sire and lost a son !
The dead are dearest, be who will alive.
Can you by filling cradles empty graves ?
But I am father, mother, both at once.
You do not understand.

BONSI.

In sooth we do,
And therefore pity ; but we still would cheer.

GROSSO.

And so do men at funerals !   Fare you well.
I thank you.   Have you sons ?   Then tell them this :

Never to wed at hey-day.   Then the blood
Surges and drowns the judgment.   For a face,
A ripple on the brow, a line, a nought,
A touch like any other, an embrace
In homely darkness scarce distinguishable,
To stamp a mortgage on your life, and be,
Like me, by folly finally foreclosed,—
Why, what is that?   The Syrens call it love,
Ulysses, lunacy, and while they sing,
Lashes his melting body to the mast,
And sails beyond them.

[Exit (right).]

VESPUCCI.

How exceeding wise !
Think you this instance might assist our boys ?

BONSI.

Nowise.   Such wit is not vicarious.
Folly is wisdom's nurse, whom we drain dry
Before we are weaned ; and other babes require
To suckle similarly.   Brought up by hand,
Lads rarely prosper.   See, across the square,
Apparently in haste, Valori comes.
On his sole will revolves the government,

Since in his cell, restrained by interdict,
Savonarola keeps.

[VALORI enters (left).]

VESPUCCI.

What news, Valori ?

VALORI.

That still this matter is not brought to term,
Which, littering yet the road, trips up the State !
The Five still live, since that each Body in turn
Shrinks from the stroke.   The Eight their guilt affirm,
Remitting judgment to the Signory,
Which, shirking a decision, calls a Court,
Formed of the Eight, with Seven of the Ten,
And five Arroti.—These unanimously
Confirm the verdict, but once more invite
The Eight to pronounce sentence.

. BONSI.

Do they shrink ?

VALORI.

Yes ; not from conscience, but from cowardice.

VESPUCCI.

Then why doth not the Signory pronounce ?

VALORI.

'Tis not their office.   That belongs the Eight,
As well you know.

BONSI.

Besides the Signory
Are hopelessly divided, four 'gainst five,
Michele Berti being Del Nero's kin,
And other three recalcitrant.

VALORI.

Wait a bit,
And see how I will spur these gibbing jades.
Be here anon, when they shall reasons give
To the assembled people why they spare
These traitors to the Commonwealth.

[CANDIDA enters (left), unnoticed by VALORI, but ob-
    served by the other two.   She advances hesi-
    tatingly towards them.]

VESPUCCI.

Fair child !
Would you have aught of us ?

[VALORI turns, and perceives CANDIDA.]

CANDIDA.

I fain would win
Signor Valori to my words awhile.

BONSI.

No difficulty there, I should surmise.
Have your occasion.

> [Exeunt VESPUCCI and BONSI (right).]

VALORI.

Speak !   I am all ear
Since you have put a bit upon my tongue
You bade me not pursue you with my vows
And so I halt.

CANDIDA.

O sir, I do not think
I ever was so scant of courtesy.
Such words would not beseem me.

VALORI.

Like to bees
Your honey lodges very near the sting,
But 'tis the second penetrates.

CANDIDA.

Forgive
If one so lowly upon one so high
Inflicted never such a trivial wound.

But let us change our parts.   'Tis I who smart,
And want your sweetness.

VALORI.

                What I have of that

Is yours irrevocably.

CANDIDA.

                I meant not that.
I come to beg, to knock, to whine, to weep,
To gain myself a passage to your heart
Through every chink of pity that you have,
And melt you into granting me.

VALORI.

                        Little need.
My heart is open, and I stand within,
Trembling, to catch your importunity.
What is it you would have ?   Quick as you ask,
'Tis given !

CANDIDA.

Lorenzo Tornabuoni's life.

VALORI.

What !   That !   That—that—is an affair of State.

I thought you some petition would prefer,
Was private, personal ?

CANDIDA.

What thing is not ?
How will you any sure distinction make
Betwixt a public and a private woe ?
What sword of execution is so fine
That it can roll rebellion in the dust,
Yet leave the rebel standing ? or what edge
Of your discriminating justice cleave
The traitor's neck, yet spare a space for love,
Unterrified, to lock its loyal arms ?
Hark ! while your ostentatious bells clang out
That retribution hath been slaked with gore,
The tear-drops widowed innocence secretes
Upon some fireless hearthstone muffled fall.
Oh ! have him respited !

VALORI.

He has no wife,
So will not leave a widow to bewail him.

CANDIDA.

And is a wife the only stay that can

P

Make life reluctant to be yoked with death?
Look!   He is flush like you, noble like you;
Like you he wears full summer in his face;
Youth dances unexhausted in his blood;
Yet you, his peer, his fellow, ay, his twin
In conscious satisfaction, thrust him out
Into the dark and famine of the night,
Just as the very banquet is prepared,
And all life's lights are shining!

VALORI.

                              You forget,
If he is young, others there be are old.
If we spare *him*, we needs must spare them all;
And to spare all would, see, be not to spare
Those they had spared not, many more than they,
Had they not in their stratagems been foiled,
And which, being spared, they quickly would renew.

CANDIDA.

I never heard you argue, sir, before.
Why do you reason now?   I'm a poor maid,
Unskilled in lunges of the tongue, and apt
Only to sue for favours.   Look!   I drop

All bootless weapons, and your mercy crave,
Mercy for *him*—for *them*, if he and they
In the same balance must be hung.

VALORI.

                         She pleads
As though she loved him !   O, you ply me hard !
But is it honest strategy to mine
My conscience with explosions in my heart,
Burrowing through its soft substance that I may ·
Feel all my solid judgments blown to space ?
I know I love in vain : but though you raise
Obstructions big as Apennine to block
My entrance to the valley of your heart,
My restless thoughts can find no rest but there,
The far-off home of fancy.   Leave me that !
Whereof I should be widowed did I think
You trafficked with my tenderness to leave
The sword of justice rusting.

CANDIDA.

                         O, I came
Sir, to importune you, but not to bribe.
Who trifle with men's honesty wear gifts
Peeping from out their sleeve; and I wear none,

Nor know what they may be.   I would corrupt
Your sternness with your gentleness, that's all.

VALORI.

That were to parley with my weaker self,
Which you yourself have strengthened.   Save for you,
I never might have learnt how deep the debt
Men owe the native atmosphere they breathe.
Forbidden to protect you, I now guard
The Commonwealth of Florence, tougher task.
Do not you turn against me, who denied
My arms a daintier duty.

CANDIDA.

How aloof
From every touch of littleness he seems !
I needs must love him now if he should speak,
And not be quite so flinty.   Then in vain
I have besought your footsteps, and must take
This pressure from your presence ?   Yet 'tis hard
That those who fain would longer live must die,
And those who willingly would die must live.
Farewell; and may your minutes never lack
The respite you refuse !

[She turns to go.]

VALORI.

"Would die," she said.
What bodes such wish ? She loves him then, 'tis plain !
Stay!   You have broken down my final fence.
If it be that you love him, own that fault,
And I will stand betwixt him and the block,
Though every throat in Florence yelled for blood,
And every visage flashed a headsman's axe.

CANDIDA.

Women love all whom grief and death attaint.

VALORI.

Save those whose grief they cause.   Why could not
    grief
Come to me from some other source than you ?
It then had drawn your pity.   When death comes,
May you be near !

CANDIDA.

I echo can that prayer,
Though may your death be far as his seems near.

VALORI.

His shall be far, and life more dead than death

Near me henceforth, so you do once aver
Your life is but a satellite to his.
I will not then extinguish it ; it shall
Shine to forfend your darkness.   But, farewell
To public honour as to private bliss.
Within his cloister, quarantined by Rome,
Savonarola scrupulously keeps,
And on my unpropped steadfastness the State
Must tower or totter ; and this ponder well,
If Florence is to stand these men must fall.
Hold back my hand from drowning them, their guilt
Will float upon a sea of innocent blood,
Freedom be chased, the Medici return,
Savonarola straight surrendered be
To the unjust inquisitors of Rome !
And this through me ! Yet, be it so !   When I
Look through your tears, the stars of duty swim,
And resolution crumbles at my feet.
Let the world crack, so your heart does not break.
I will go hide me where the panther hides,
In jungles where fame comes not, nor reproach
Can christen fondness with a fouler name.
Confess you love him !

CANDIDA (*aside*).

　　　　　　　Why does this close word

Pursue my footsteps, double as I will ?

VALORI.

Why do you hesitate ?　One breath from you

Will save him, but it must be uttered quick.

> [People enter the Piazza. The doors of the Palazzo Pub-
> blico are thrown open. The SIGNORY, followed
> by the OTTO DI BALÌA, the DIECI DE GUERRA, and
> their attendants, also the TWELVE BUONI UOMINI,
> the SIXTEEN GONFALONIERI of the COMPANIES,
> and the EIGHTY, or SENATE, come out, and pre-
> pare to take their places on the benches in the
> Loggia de' Lanzi. CANDIDA is standing at the
> left corner of the stage, near the footlights. VALORI
> goes nearer to her. At the same time, a scaffold
> is wheeled forward and stands between the Palazzo
> Pubblico and the Fountain in the Piazza. A veiled
> Headsman mounts, and stands immovable, a naked
> axe reposing on his shoulder.]

VALORI.

If from the scaffold I now pluck him back,

Will you his rescued sensitiveness take

To the warm refuge of encircling arms ?

Speak! for the murderous seconds will not wait !

Either the earth or yours must be his bed.

Quick! quick! Pronounce!

CANDIDA.

Then ne must die!

[LETIZIA enters (left).]

VALORI.

[To LETIZIA.

Fair maid,

See to this lady!

[LETIZIA leads CANDIDA away.   Exeunt (left).]

SCENE X.

[The SIGNORY sit upon a bench outside the Palazzo Pubblico.
The OTTO DI BALÌA, the DIECI DI GUERRA, and the
EIGHTY, or SENATE, are seated on benches in the Loggia
de' Lanzi.   On the floor of the stage, facing them in a semi-
circle, are ranged the TWELVE BUONI UOMINI, the SIX-
TEEN GONFALONIERI of the COMPANIES, and the persons
forming the TWELVE PANCATE of the simple citizens. Behind these, and to right and left of them, stand the Crowd.
The scaffold rises, as described above.   VALORI occupies
the centre of the stage.   FRANCESCO GUALTEROTTI, one
of the Dieci de Guerra, rises.]

GUALTEROTTI.

Signors and Citizens!
The safety of the Commonwealth demands

Delay be ended, and the guilty pay
The forfeit of their lives.

VOICES.

                              Appeal! Appeal!
Let the Grand Council speak.

GUALTEROTTI.

                              Wherefore appeal,
When every voice hath spoken that the law
Appoints to speak?   Have not the Signory
With them the Eight, the Doctors of the Law
The panels of the citizens, and, last,
Two hundred special jurymen, pronounced
Their guilt is plain?

FRANCESCO DEGLI ALBIZZI.

                      Let justice quick be done!
Justice, I say!   Than justice, nothing less!

   [A Messenger enters the Square, carrying written documents.]

VALORI.

What bring you there?

                      [He takes the documents, and opens them.]

VALORI.

See!   Want you farther proof,
Signors and Citizens, that there is need
Of expedition, it is written down
In these official messages despatched
From Rome and Milan.   Your ambassadors
Unravel farther Medicean toils,
Abetted by the Borgian Pope, to snare
The liberties of Florence.

[Hands the documents to the SIGNORY.]

VOICES.

No appeal!

SOME VOICES.

Yes! the Grand Council.   Let the People speak.

VALORI.

The People have been heard, and are heard now.
Want you the execution?

[To the People.]

THE CROWD.

Ay! and straight!

A GONFALONIERE.

And if we do not get it, we will bring

The gonfalons of all the Companies
Into the streets, and wake the very stones
Against the traitors.

ONE OF THE EIGHT.

But we have convinced
The Five of treason, and we but await
The pleasure of the Signory, to pass
A fitting sentence.

[Sits down.]

    [VALORI, with furious mien and fast footsteps, strides to
the table in front of the bench where the nine
members of the SIGNORY are sitting, and seizes the
ballot-box, saying at the same time :]

VALORI.

Only one is fit,
And, it pronounced not, scandal will ensue.

    [Turning fiercely to LUCA MARTINI, one of the SIGNORY,
who is Proposto for the day, and holding out to him
the ballot-box.]

VALORI.

You, the Proposto, put it to the vote.
Your vacillating slowness lets the State
Slide down the jaws of ruin.

[LUCA MARTINI hands the ballot-box to the other members of the SIGNORY, who drop their balls into it,
and he then returns it to VALORI, who counts the
balls.]

VALORI.

Still but five !

Now to what end, O potent Signors,

Have ye so many citizens convened

Who by the hand of your own notary

Have signified their judgment 'gainst these Five,

Subverters of the freedom of the State,

And enemies of Florence ?

[The Five Prisoners are led into the Piazza, barefoot and
in chains, to move the compassion of the People.
VALORI turns his back upon them, and addresses
the SIGNORY more violently than before.]

VALORI.

Have you grown deaf,

And do not catch the universal cry

Jealous to save the Commonwealth, or blind,

And from your lofty watch-towers not discern,

The imminence of peril ?   Mind you, sirs !

The People placed you where you are, to shield

Those liberties which, through a false respect

For citizens in bloody treasons dyed,

You have uncovered.   But of this be sure,

> [He unsheaths his sword.]

An arm will not be wanting, wanting never,

To guard so just and sanctified a Cause

'Gainst them that traverse it !   Now, vote again.

> [LUCA MARTINI again hands round the ballot-box. As he
> does so, the prisoners advance to the foot of the
> scaffold.   BERNARDO DEL NERO mounts the steps,
> reaches the summit, and stands on one side of
> the block.   NICCOLÒ RIDOLFI follows, and takes
> his place on the other side of the block.   LORENZO
> TORNABUONI begins to ascend, but as he reaches
> the fifth step, there is a shout, and he pauses and
> turns, facing (left).   At that moment, CANDIDA
> re-enters, accompanied by LETIZIA.]

MARTINI.

Our voices are unanimous for death.

ONE OF THE EIGHT.

Therefore be death their doom !

> [The People shout, " Long live the Commonwealth !
> Long live Liberty ! " TORNABUONI gazes at CAN-
> DIDA, who veils her eyes, and then ascends the re-
> maining steps.   VALORI, still with sword lifted,
> turns and sees CANDIDA.   He inverts his sword,
> and gazes on the ground.   The curtain falls.]

END OF ACT III.

ACT IV.

SCENE I.

Piazza of the Duomo. On the Side Towards The Baptistery.

[The Bell of the Campanile of Giotto tolls at intervals. A bier is carried slowly across the stage (from right to left), on the shoulders of four members of the MISERICORDIA, clad in the long black cloak and hood of the Order, only their eyes being visible. A few persons of the poorer class are sitting on the steps of the Duomo, or leaning against the Baptistery; the women knitting, and some children playing near them. DOFFO SPINI and young SODERINI enter (left) as the bier moves on. They make way for it, come nearer the footlights, and watch it till it passes.]

SODERINI.

A wintry emblem for an April day.

SPINI.

The season keeps its promise, sun and shower.

SODERINI.

Here showers, mostly.   Would that I were back

In the Valdarno, left but yesterday;
For there the spring, in brand-new buskin green,
And fledged with shafts in glittering sunshine dipped,
Was hunting wolfish winter from the plain.
Plague on the city, with its doleful dong,
And following funerals !

[A nightingale sings.]

SPINI.

Hark !   Heard you that ?

It was the nightingale, that all day long
Now in the gardens of the city sings.
Death troubles not his note.

SODERINI.

I have been told

By homely folk he sings unto his mate
As she keeps close on her mysterious nest.
I ween he fluteth only to himself,
Because his throat is full.   Poets were wise
To copy his example, and to sing
Despite of darkness, and though all ears sleep.

SPINI.

How wise you wax, if wise is to be sad.

SODERINI.

Wisdom and sadness are as near, blithe youth,
As sun and shade.   Would it were otherwise!
Experience, feeding upon all life's sweets,

[Bell tolls.]

Itself turns sour.   But see! they come again!

> [Another litter, but empty, borne by the MISERICORDIA,
>   passes across the stage (from right to left), followed
>   by BARTOLOMMEO CEI, who remains with SPINI
>   and SODERINI.]

SPINI.

Whom with their sable paces fetch they now?

CEI.

The lustiest lad that ever wound an arm
Round the shy dimples of a lissom waist:
A faun to dance, a dryad at delight,
Whereof he drained and drained, and found no dregs.
Pallone knew no brawnier wrist than his;
And skimming like a swallow through the chase,
Nor needing e'er to perch, he looked to live
Upon the bounty of the air, and bring
The summer with him.

SODERINI.

Is he dead?

CEI.

Alack!

His flight is over, his expansion done,
His goodly sinews, florid lineaments,
Outlooking youth with fair hopes ringleted,
Packed in a coffin! O thou wanton thief,
That stealest all things, and that art withal
No richer for thy thefts, why canst not leave
Beauty that makes thee no more beautiful,
And spare that love which, when thou hast purloined,
We only hate thee more!

SPINI.

Come, come! Cheer up!
You are as moral as that passing-bell,
And as monotonous. Change but the peal,
The self-same clapper, differently swung,
Will put us all in heart. 'Tis true, the Plague
Hath thinned the ranks of goodly fellowship;
But many a churl hath likewise closed his chops;
And since all suffer, all are ill-content,
And probe the origin!

CEI.

'Tis easy named.
'Tis Frà Girolamo, whose gnawing tongue
Hath eaten deep into the Commonwealth.

SPINI.

Keep grinding on that point, and screw it home.
Mark, Soderini! it already bites.
While you, in broken covert, pike on hip,
Were lithely jousting at the wild boar's tusk,
The hunter's work in Florence was not stayed.
At length we count a friendly Signory,
Whereof the Gonfaloniere is
Pietro Pepoleschi.   With him works
Giovanni Berlinghieri; and the Eight
Go mostly 'gainst the Friar.

SODERINI.

Hopeful news,
As April is until November comes;
But this complexion in two months may change.

SPINI.

Ere those months be as though they never were,

This melancholy monk shall fly our walls,
And Florence have her joyance back again.
O, 'tis a trap well baited.   Set a thief
The adage says, if you a thief would snare ;
And I say, set a monk to catch a monk.

CEI.

But catch your first monk first.

SPINI.

And that we have.
A lean Franciscan, in the Lent just gone,
Preaching in Santa Croce, and egged on
By Frà Mariano, publicly announced
His readiness to traverse flaming share
With Frà Girolamo, and thus decide
Who of the twain teach doctrine orthodox.

SODERINI.

The fool would soon be proved a heretic,
And burnt before his time.

SPINI.

Not quite so fast.
A fool in folly easy is outdone.

The children's plaything, Frà Domenico,
Savanarola's shadow, quickly snatched
The challenge from the rash Franciscan's mouth,
Who forthwith mumbled that his quarrel lay
Not with the follower, but the Master's self.
He, chiding Frà Domenico, had fain
The test eluded; but the Signory
Stuck his Conclusions on the city walls,
Inviting all to uphold or contravene
By Ordeal of Fire.   Forthwith each cowl
That bobs within San Marco notified
Its wish to have a singeing.   O! 'tis rare,
This glueing of these rooks with their own lime.

SODERINI.

Will the Franciscans stick?

SPINI.

      Our only fear.
But Frà Mariano, primed by Rome, as yet
Keeps their faint faces forward, whispering them
They need not fear the Ordeal, which is framed
But as a pit for Frà Girolamo,
Who, entering once the flames, will straight be burnt,

Or, entering not, will live discredited.

Beside, the very Piagnoni cry

The loudest for a miracle, while he

With verity his visions so confounds,

He fancies air, fire, water, earth, will prove

To wand of faith subservient elements.

SODERINI.

They say he is to preach again.   Is 't true ?

SPINI.

[Pointing to the pulpit outside the Duomo.]

Look!   All the gear is ready.   He will preach

This day at noon; a sign he 's desperate.

But being still excommunicated, thus

He will but more exasperate the Pope,

Who even now forbids the embarrassed State

To raise one soldo from the Church, unless

This shorn heresiarch be despatched alive

Into his hands.

CEI.

What says the Signory ?

SPINI.

To this no chance it ever will assent.

He by adoption is a Florentine,

And Florence cannot duck its knees to Rome.

So we ourselves must play the Pope, and be

Judges of orthodoxy.   Mind you both

Be here at noon.   Defenders of the Faith

Will all be wanted.

CEI.

'Tis a novel part,

And your demands grow enigmatical.

SPINI.

Have I not told you Frà Girolamo

Is going to preach?   The Compagnacci, too,

Will be upon the ground to serenade

The sermon with some singing.   Do not fail

To swell the chorus.   It is time I went

To tune my instruments.

[Exit (left).]

SCENE II.

[The Funeral Bell again tolls.   Groups of PIAGNONI and ARRAB-
      BIATI come into the Square.]

FIRST PIAGNONE.

                                    I say it is.

Ask you these gentlemen.

FIRST ARRABBIATO.

                              Forgive me, sir !

But is it true the Ordeal of Fire

Is coming off to-day ?

SODERINI.

                    The gossip jogs,

'Tis fixed for Vespers; and if I were you,

I would not miss the roasting.   Come along !

                              [He takes CEI's arm.]

Leave these plebeian pundits to decide

Which is for Francis, which for Dominick.

The ignorant love argument.

      [Exeunt (left).   Another litter, carried by the MISERI-
            CORDIA, passes ; and the bell again tolls, but the
            People take no heed.]

FIRST PIAGNONE.

> Told you so.

FIRST ARRABBIATO.

Told us what?

SECOND PIAGNONE.

> That Frà Domenico
> Will walk into the flames and not be burnt.

SECOND ARRABBIATO.

Frà Giuliano, the Franciscan monk,
Will brave it too, and be as little hurt.

THIRD ARRABBIATO.

But will that stop the plague ?

FOURTH ARRABBIATO.

> Or 'chance reduce
> The price of grain, and make a crazia weigh
> A trifle heavier ?

FIRST ARRABBIATO.

> Faith ! and will it lift
> From our curved backs the burden of one tax ?

Will it recover Pisa, or relieve
The granaries of Leghorn idly stored?
That's what I ask.

FIRST PIAGNONE.

   You fellows have no faith.
Why, Frà Girolamo has promised us
Relief from all things, so we only wait.

  [Another coffin is carried past, the bell again tolling.]

SECOND ARRABBIATO.

      [Pointing to the bier.]
He has done waiting; and so soon shall we,
If things in Florence long go on like this.
Half of us die, and those that die not starve;
And when faith neither feeds nor keeps alive,
It's shadowy stuff.

SECOND PIAGNONE.

   But if the flames should spare
The champion of Saint Mark, yet leave their seam
On the Franciscan, surely 'twill be plain
That Heaven with Frà Girolamo agrees,
And what he says is true?

FIRST ARRABBIATO.

                    I'll answer "if,"
When water fails to quench and fire to burn.

SECOND ARRABBIATO.

He has promised us a miracle so long,
We want to see one.

FIRST PIAGNONE.

                    Faith ! and so do we,
And that is why we press the Ordeal.
It is not we who shrink.

THIRD ARRABBIATO.

                    Who is it, then ?

SECOND PIAGNONE.

Not Frà Girolamo.   Why, every monk
Within Saint Mark is——

FOURTH ARRABBIATO.

                    Burning to be burnt.
                              [They all laugh.]

SECOND PIAGNONE.

I said not so, but rather that they burn——

FIRST ARRABBIATO.

To prove by burning that they will not burn.

> [They laugh again.]

SECOND ARRABBIATO.

Well, let us have the Ordeal !

FIRST PIAGNONE

> That you shall ;

For Frà Silvestro had a dream wherein

He saw his brother monk come out unscathed.

THIRD ARRABBIATO.

Enough of dreams ! we want realities.

French Charles has come and gone, and not come

> back,

And Pisa, too, has gone, and not come back.

What boot these constant prophesyings ?   If

Savonarola be inspired,—well then,

Now is the time to show it.   If he be not,

Let us be done with sermons.

VOICES.

> That's the test.

A miracle !   A miracle !   We want

An argument that's palpable.

FIRST PIAGNONE.

                            But look,

Look what a lovely litter comes this way !

A maiden on her bier ; her golden hair,

That keeps the only show of life she hath,

Droops o'er the darksome drapery ; her hands,

Crossed in unconscious modesty, repose

Upon her bosom where love heaves no more.

Her arteries are quiet cloisters now,

Where no one even prays ; her tapering limbs

Stretch on the couch, material, meaningless.

White, white from head to foot ; and under each

Are cyclamens and lilies.   'Tis a sight

Far too significant for kindred life

To look on long.

FIRST ARRABBIATO.

                    Know you not who it is ?

It is the fair Letizia, good as fair,

The sweet one of Bettuccio, ah ! too sweet

For him or any other !   Tasteless death

Hath got that morsel now.

SECOND PIAGNONE.

                            And who is that,

Walking upon the off side of the bier ?

SECOND ARRABBIATO.

That is Bettuccio. Don't you see him plain
Sobbing beneath his funeral domino?
That will be Grosso, on the hither side,
Who modelled her so often;—marble now
Both copy and original. His wife
Will rail upon her comeliness no more.
She still is 'mong the quick?

THIRD ARRABBIATO.

Aye, very quick.
Dog eats not dog, and plague feeds not on plague.

FOURTH ARRABBIATO.

Her brother props behind; but who the fourth,
Whose scabbard peeps from out his ebon gown,
I can surmise not. The girl's birth was plain,
While he is labelled noble by his sword.

SECOND PIAGNONE.

Made nobler, carrying her. Besides, good friend,
Death is a democrat who levels all.

[The bier with the body of LETIZIA passes away (left),
and MARCUCCIO SALVIATI, surrounded by a band
of armed PIAGNONI, is seen to be in the Square.

He ranges them near the pulpit, which they surround.　He himself joins the persons who are con-
versing.　Several unarmed PIAGNONI, women and
children among them, come into the Piazza of the
Duomo, and some of them gather round SALVIATI.]

FIRST ARRABBIATO.

So then, he really is about to preach ?

SALVIATI.

You soon will see.　For six slow months his lips
Have by the Interdict been frozen up ?

FIRST PIAGNONE.

Has Rome then thawed ?

SALVIATI.

　　　　　　　No, but his own voice hath ;
And from that source such eloquence will flow
That it our fortunes once again will float.

SECOND ARRABBIATO.

Heard you Frà Mariano yesterday,
Outside the Agostiniani, preach ?

THIRD ARRABBIATO.

Lord ! how he thumped !

SECOND PIAGNONE.

          'Twas contumacious stuff,
Less worthy of the pulpit than the wharf.
The very scavengers their stomachs turned
From such a surfeit of raw violence.

THIRD PIAGNONE.

And much it stood him; for this very morn,
A deputation clamoured at Saint Mark's,
Imploring Frà Girolamo once more
To face the people.

      [DOFFO SPINI, attended by SODERINI and CEI, and
        followed by armed COMPAGNACCI, enter (right).
        They seem surprised the space near the pulpit is
        already occupied by the PIAGNONI. SALVIATI makes
        a sign to his followers to hold their ground. SPINI
        and his followers cross the stage, and range them-
        selves in a semicircle (left).]

FIRST ARRABBIATO.

          Let him face them then.
Monsignor Lionardo warns us all
Not to attend.

FIRST PIAGNONE.

He is a Medici.

SECOND ARRABBIATO.

But none the less Archbishop of this See.

The Excommunication lately launched

Is by his orders being again affixed

To every church in Florence.

VOICES OF PIAGNONI.

> Tear it down !

SPINI.

A shrewd device.   Paste paper o'er the sun,

And vow it does not shine.   As though we had

Not foes enough already in the League

Of Milan, Venice, Naples, Florence must

Secure the astute hostility of Rome ;

And all because a friar will not consent

To stick to paternosters.

> [Shouting is heard. SALVIATI hurries to the back of
> the stage. Crowds of people come on. SAVONA-
> ROLA, attended by FRÀ DOMENICO and other
> Monks, makes his appearance, guarded by more
> armed PIAGNONI, and ascends the pulpit, well sur-
> rounded by SALVIATI's band. The COMPAGNACCI
> get as close as possible. The Crowd distributes
> itself where it can.]

FIRST PIAGNONE.

> See ! he comes.

SECOND PIAGNONE.

> This way! this way!
We shall hear perfectly.

> [SAVONAROLA kneels, and prays before a crucifix,
> which stands on the ledge of the pulpit.]

SECOND PIAGNONE.

How hollow and inanimate he looks,
As though the skin were stretched upon the bone.

FIRST PIAGNONE.

Wait till he speaks, he then will seem alive;
Tighter the parchment, louder sounds the drum.

SECOND PIAGNONE.

The lines have even deepened in his brow
Since Frà Bartolommeo limned his head.
The temples and the jutting cheek-bones loom
Unnaturally large, and the sunk eyes
Have, like a spent volcano, fallen in,
Leaving dark hollowness where once was fire.
The fingers, thin and fanciful, proclaim
Vigil, and fast, and prayer.

THIRD PIAGNONE.

> What would you have?

The cloister, when its weeds are rightly donned,
Is an anticipation of the grave.
Its hymns are dirges, and its sackcloth folds
Premature cerements.

FOURTH PIAGNONE.

Hush! he is going to speak.

[SAVONAROLA rises.]

SAVONAROLA.

Servants of God! God's servant, here I stand
Under the canopy of God once more.
Why have I come? To tell you nothing new,
But reaffirm the ancient messages,
Declared to you so often. If I retract
One syllable of teaching, stone me straight,
And drive me from this pulpit.

[There is a slight commotion on the side where the
COMPAGNACCI stand; but it subsides.]

SAVONAROLA.

This is Thine,
This is Thy city, O Lord! Thine is it still,
This city of Florence, chosen by Thee, and blest,
Illuminating it afresh with faith

And manners purified : first, heavenly gifts,

With gifts of earth to follow ; chief of all,

Recovered liberty.　Time was you crouched

Under the government of One, who said

Pay, and you paid ; barter your daughters here,

And to unwilling nuptials were they forced ;

Do ill, and ill from very fear you did.

But Christ delivered you, for Christ it was

Who drove the Medici from out your walls,

Bade the French King depart, and to you then

Gave the Grand Council, key and corner-stone

Of civic freedom.　Pay then tax to Christ,

Your King, your Liberator, who demands

Impost of virtue, chastity, faith, prayer,

All that this life impoverish not, and rich

Will make the life to come.

> [Suddenly a bomb explodes, drums are beaten, and disorder and confusion arise.　Women scream, some fly from the place ; and the COMPAGNACCI, drawing their swords, strive to get near to the pulpit.　But MARCUCCIO SALVIATI and his armed PIAGNONI, present a determined front, and after a little the disorder subsides.　SAVONAROLA, who has not moved from the pulpit, now holds aloft a crucifix.]

SAVONAROLA.

Look on this !

Trust it, and fear not.   There are those who say

That excommunications have been launched.

What excommunications?   As for me,

I would that such were carried on a lance

All through the streets of Florence; weapons apt

'Gainst evil-doers and heresiarchs,

Not against those who struggle to reform

The Church of Christ.   Who is it, late in Rome,

Hath lost a son, by his own brother slain

In a lewd quarrel?   Would you know the way

To make this excommunication void?

> [He strikes two keys together. The Crowd laugh. Then,
> growing terribly serious again, he continues.]

SAVONAROLA.

If I this excommunication pray

To have removed from me, then, Lord, prepare

A pit for me in Hell!

FIRST PIAGNONE.

He looks inspired.

I did not deem that a terrestrial tongue

Could sound so heavenly.

SECOND PIAGNONE.

Hush!   He speaks anew!

SAVONAROLA.

This excommunication comes from Rome :

From Rome that spends its nights in harlotries,

Its noons in gossiping in choir, and turns

Altars to counters whereon gold may chink.

Upon the seat of Solomon it sits,

Provoking all that pass.   It multiplies

In Italy, in France, in Spain—where not ?—

Its fornications.   Out with thy sword, O Lord,

And smite this ribald meretricious Church,

Its palaces, its pomp !   Thy justice flash,

And give it up to hatred !   Horses and dogs,

Courtiers and trappings, perfumes, tapestries,

Is this the Church of God ?   All things they sell,

Marriage and masses, pardons, benefices;

And excommunicate who will not buy.

I will not buy their favour.   Lord, Thou knowest

These things I want not, but Thy Cross, Thy Cross.

God and the Virgin, Angels and the Saints,

I call to witness that the things revealed,

And verified divinely, were inspired

In those long vigils of the night endured

For those who turn against me.

> [Again there is disturbance in the Crowd; but MAR-

CUCCIO SALVIATI and the PIAGNONI barricade the
approaches to the pulpit with their bodies.   During
this interval occurs the following dialogue.]

FIRST PIAGNONE.

       Who can doubt

He is a Prophet ?

SECOND PIAGNONE.

     He whirls me like a wind

That will not let the loose leaves lag behind,

But drives them further forward than itself.

SAVONAROLA.

      What do they want,.

The false informers, they that have provoked

This excommunication?   To destroy

Freedom of government, and in its place

Establish riotous living, luxury, vice,

The pandars of the despot!   You desire

That Leghorn were relieved.   Yourselves relieve

Of Satan's armies that invest your souls,

And Pisa to subjection will return.

Christ is your king, and not the Medici.

He hath command in chief, and you must use

The strategy of virtue.   If for this
My soul be excommunicated here—
Yet not in Heaven!   Thou, O dear Lord, didst die
For my sake, and I fain would die for Thine.
Cause them to persecute me ; let me not
Die in my bed !   For never have I ceased,
Through fear of men, from preaching.   Take my life,
As Thine was taken.   Grant me martyrdom,
And Florence resurrection !

> [SAVONAROLA turns to descend from the pulpit.   But
> voices on every side, proceeding both from the
> COMPAGNACCI and the PIAGNONI, cry out.]

VOICES.

But the Fire!

How, Ser Girolamo, about the Fire,
The promised Ordeal?

SAVONAROLA.

Who promised it?
Think you I have so mean a task to do,
That I in trivial wrangles will be meshed?
What needs the spirit with these material tests?
Let them confute our doctrines, be they false,
And prove me excommunicated.   Else,

I am not answered.   As for prophecies,

I gave them at their value, and impose

Credence on no one; for my sole intent

Was to convert you unto godly lives,

And this needs fire, the fire of charity,

The miracle of faith.   The rest is nothing.

> [There are murmurs of disapprobation.   People in the
> Crowd speak to each other, shrug their shoulders,
> and gesticulate.]

SAVONAROLA.

What is it you desire ?   'Tis said our foes

Are ready for the flames.   And so are we,

If it be for God's honour; and of this

An instant doubt not, that if those who feel

Truly inspired of Heaven confront the flame,

Out of its clutches they untouched shall come,

And not a nerve be shrivelled.   If it take place,—

The which I know not.   God knows.   As for me,

I must reserve myself for serious work,

In fertilising which, empty my life,

Till none of it be left.   Lord! take it all !

But this I tell you, miracles will come,

And portents supernatural amaze

The sensual and incredulous.   O God !

Stultify not Thy servant, but be quick

And sound the hour !

> [SAVONAROLA descends from the pulpit. As he does so,
> DOFFO SPINI and the COMPAGNACCI again strive
> to force their way to it, evidently intending violence
> to SAVONAROLA. But MARCUCCIO SALVIATI and
> his followers maintain their ground, though a
> struggle takes place, and surround and protect
> SAVONAROLA as he returns to San Marco.]

FIRST PIAGNONE.

How I wish

I could get nearer !

SECOND PIAGNONE.

Even armèd men

Could scarce in so confused an hour as this

Have contact with the Prior.   How they sway

And rock against each other !   There are some

Would Frà Girolamo assassinate,

Could they but penetrate to striking-point.

No fear to-day.

FIRST PIAGNONE.

Nor any day, so long

As God sustains him.

> [SAVONAROLA and his Attendants, the ARRABBIATI,

PIAGNONI, COMPAGNACCI, and the Crowd, gradually pass off the stage in various directions.   The
scene is shifted.]

SCENE III.

A Street in Florence.

[Enter Luca Corsini and Domenico Bonsi (left),
Guidantonio Vespucci (right).]

CORSINI.

Well met, Vespucci.   Do you bring us news
Of the last sitting of the Signory?

VESPUCCI.

Yes ; and news sensible.   They place a gag
Upon the Friar.   He is to preach no more.

BONSI.

He preached a sermon now to wake the dead
And vivify the stones.   'Twere time he ceased.
Helpful to chase the Medici, he blocks
The way to sober government, that is,
And ever was, the appanage of few.

VESPUCCI.

Was he heard plausibly?

CORSINI.

Two different streams
Contended for the current; but 'twas plain
The adverse had it.

BONSI.

That, undoubtedly.
But for Marcuccio Salviati's folk,
Who elbowed them aside, the crowd had plucked
His cassock somewhat rudely.

VESPUCCI.

Who can wonder?
For all his prophecies have come to nought.
Famine and pestilence are at their doors
Posted like sentinels, and challenge all,
Save death and hunger, that demand to pass.
This for their private woes.   The public ills
Are not more few nor less accountable.
All round Volterra desolation spreads,
As an unhealthy fungus doth its spawn,

In ever-widening circles.   Pescia grows
Its harvest for our foes ; the Pisans scour,
Unhindered, the Maremma ; and the ships
Of Venice still from Leghorn cut as off.

CORSINI.

Heard you a letter seriously shaped,
Despatched by Frà Girolamo to Charles,
Was by Il Moro seized upon the way ?

BONSI.

They vouch me it contains a solemn prayer
The King a General Council would convene
To render the last conclave void and null,
Pluck the Tiara from the Borgia's head,
And give another Pope to Christendom.

VESPUCCI.

Aye, and that Ludovico hath consigned
The bold petition to the Pontiff's hands.

CORSINI.

An accident more likely to succeed,
Than many a deft design.   Take this for sure :

When chance conspires against a man, his days
Of eminence are numbered.   In this world,
That grows its crop of courtiers by the hour,
There never was so rank a sycophant
As this same Fortune.

VESPUCCI.

                    I was homeward bound
Unto the midday meal, a while delayed
By the irregular motion of these times.
I pray you share it with me.

BONSI.

                    Willingly,
Where we may then more leisurely discourse
Of the immediate symptoms of the State,
And what should be their medicine.

CORSINI.

                    After you.

[Exeunt (left).   As they do so, enter CANDIDA (right),
          and tries one of the doors.]

SCENE IV.

CANDIDA (alone).

Not yet returned!   He lingers by the grave,
Whose cold insensate pressure hardens round
The unresisting softness his void arms
Were wont to fondle!   In the light of death
Love grows intelligible.   Love is loss,
Or that which we might lose, and I have lost
What I was careful not enough to keep,
Since, through some shyness in the blood, afraid
To note I had it, till I had it not.
Yet were I now the comfort of some heart
That, like to mine, craves to be comforted,
I might Letizia's or Bettuccio's fate
Invite, which now I baffle, being alone.
Came death, it me would wrench from no one's arms,
Nor leave a bleeding branch.   Alas! poor youth!
He is one rent; lest he should drip to death,
Some styptic must be found.   I would have coaxed
His footsteps from her tomb, had custom left
Open that avenue; but 'tis ordained,

In death, as sooth in every pinch of life,
That women, lest they cry too loud, must hug
Their agony in silence.

    [Enter a figure (left), draped in the robes of the MISERI-
       CORDIA.]

CANDIDA.

Here is one
Perchance can second me.   Forgive me, sir,
But since you wear the draperies of death,
You chance can tell me if the charnel hath
Closed its stiff hinges on the final jaunt
Of her they called Letizia ?

DRAPED FIGURE.

She is urned
In the damp cells of subterranean sleep,
And never more will net the April wind,
Nor mirror glancing summer in her cheek.
Her ways are nothingness.

CANDIDA.

And he, to whom
They late were all ?

DRAPED FIGURE.

A pitiable sight !
He plunged against the hard unyielding earth,
As though it were another element,
And he by dint of forcible wide arms
Could dive to where she had been plummeted.
Recovered from that fancy, he repaired
Straight to San Marco, resolutè to don
The garb of Dominick.

CANDIDA.

O well resolved !
And it will put a crown on her content,
In that far Paradise where now she dwells,
To have him thus so near her.   When he dies
Their union will be instant.

DRAPED FIGURE.

You predict
As one who knew them well.

CANDIDA.

And well I did.
She was the lovingest maiden ever lisped,

And he the round fulfilment of her dream.

I cannot think of them apart ; they were,

If dual, only in the double sense

That all things are which you may cleave in twain,

As death awhile hath cleft them.

DRAPED FIGURE.

Happy pair,

To have known unity, that aching quest

Of conscious fragments !

CANDIDA.

Have *you* lost it too ?

Whoe'er you be, my pity wells to you.

DRAPED FIGURE.

Alack ! I never had that prize to lose.

There was a maiden, as it might be you,

And truly not less comely,—can you bear

The praises of another in your ear,—

Who might have made my oneness, and would not.

CANDIDA.

That sounds unlike ; for though I cannot scan

Your aspect under that disfavouring robe,

'Tis like an instinct to surmise of one
Whose speech is fair, his seeming were not foul.

DRAPED FIGURE.

Ah! fair and foul in love are close allied!
Spring in her eyes, but winter in her heart,
She coaxed the frail white blossom of love to show,
Then with a frost untimely nipped it black.

CANDIDA.

I pray you then, compare me not with her:
I never had done that.

DRAPED FIGURE.

[Throwing aside the dress of the MISERICORDIA.]
Who did it, then?

CANDIDA.

Valori!
[VALORI stands motionless, and both are silent.   Then
CANDIDA resumes.]
Upon *me* you charge that sin!
If such offence unwomanly were mine,
I would not check contrition.   But O, sir!
True as I am a maiden, ne'er with guile,
Nor any knowledge of the thing I did,

Entangled I your fancy.　Even now
I am of instinct destitute to know
What in me dwelleth to make you complete ;
Or rather dwelt :—for 'tis the past you chide,
And, being the past, 'tis easily forgot.

VALORI.

There is no past in such a love as mine,
But a perpetual present, foiling time ;
And but for some poor service to the State,
Poor but persistent, its unanswered want
Had questioned my existence.　As it is,
It follows me like silence, which we note
Only when hubbub ceases.　Fare you well !
My homage linger with you !　Public cares
Exact me now.

CANDIDA.

　　　　　Can they one moment spare,
One minute of your life before you go ?
Am I unmaidenly ?　But there is that
Which I would fain deliver, knew I how.
You spoke of homage ; homage is to you,
And I am choking with it.　You are great,
Far—fixed—magnanimous, I know not what,

For I have but a girl's vocabulary,

But that which women venerate and admire,

Think noble, mark of manly masterdom :

You understand me—don't you ?—tell me, sir !

VALORI.

I understand you, maiden, very well.

You give me hugely more than is my due,

But infinitely less than is my want.

You exile me to Heaven, while all I craved

Was one near touch of earthly tenderness.

I thank you, but I pray you let me go,

Or I shall but again untune my mind,

Strung by restraint to active harmony,

By dwelling on that chord.   Respect me still ;

'Tis all that I can hope for in this sphere.

CANDIDA.

Now, now, you grow too manly !   Reverence, fear,

Praise inarticulate, bold reluctancy,—

Why, what are these ?   There is a word—a word—

I do not think I know it, though your lips

Have framed it often—will you help me not ?—

A word—a word—out with it then !—'tis Love !

[He opens his arms, and she sinks into them.]

VALORI.

True ?　Is it true ?　Then love me as Love loves :
Let the heart's fervour rush up to the lips,
And bubble over !　Is it long, sweet life,
That you have known this secret ?

CANDIDA.

　　　　　　　　Only now !
Love's way with us and you is different.
You mind me of the swallow that is here
To-day, and all at once, that yesterday
Was nowhere to be seen, so swift he comes ;
While we are like the lilac-tips, and bud
For a provoking season ere we break.
We dream, not even knowing that we dream,
Up to the very moment we awake.

VALORI.

And you have woke ?

CANDIDA.

　　　　　O yes ! to find it day.
But I must not monopolise my sun.
The State, I know, hath need of you.　It was

In noting how you love her, that I learnt
To—tell me how you call it;

VALORI.

> Learnt to love,

As I love you!

CANDIDA.

> How well you guess my thought!

Only—is this not so?—there is no love,
That merits such high christening, but is built
Firm upon some foundation out of sight;
God, country, virtue, something not ourself,
To which ourself is nothing, save the proof
Of its invisible sureness.

VALORI.

> You recall

The savour of our colloquy that night—
Do you remember?—when the shooting stars
Trailed you a text for holy homily.
Nor shall we lack the sanction, love, you seek.
The peril of the Commonwealth is close.
Alone I had to fence it through the months
Savonarola still forbore to preach.

His voice is now inhibited again,
And this time by the Signory.   The crowd,
Gross misinterpreters of subtle speech,
And sturdy for the tangible, demand
A miracle, a portent, some plain proof
That Heaven is his confederate.

CANDIDA.

It will come,
If it be needed.

VALORI.

Who will know the need?

CANDIDA.

Why, He who knoweth all things.   Be at peace.

VALORI.

I do not like this Ordeal of Fire.
It is a lure devised to ruin him :
A touchstone, whereby tested, never cause
Yet was, but did betray too much alloy.
It is a worldlier world, love, than you think;
Where Virtue drowns because it cannot swim,
While dexterous Vice rides buoyant on the wave,
Because it knows the trick.

CANDIDA.

                    Yet there was One
Whose divine virtue walked upon the waves.
Trust Him and your strong deeds.

VALORI.

                    And your soft ·voice.

CANDIDA.

Nay, never trust to that!   I am not yet
What love and you must make me.   I will strive,
By clasping as the ivy clasps, to climb
As high as that it clings to.

VALORI.

                    Clasp it now,
No parasite, but with thy leaning love
Buttress life's lofty purposes.   But see,
Your words have made me——

CANDIDA.

                    Never fear to weep;
For tears are summer showers to the soul,
To keep it fresh and green; gathering no more,

The shrivelled leaves of faith and fancy fall,
And winter settles on a waning life.

VALORI.

O my delicious April, never cease
To weep and smile at once !

[Persiane are flung back, doors are thrown open, and
there are signs of afternoon.]

CANDIDA.

But see, the streets,
Midday siesta over, 'gin to stir
With common life; and this uncommon joy
Must at the harsh stroke of familiar things
Own its brief hour concluded.   There!   Farewell !

VALORI.

But whither do you go ?

CANDIDA.

Can you not guess!
To render thanks for this felicity,
Within my votive chapel in Saint Mark's,
Whose Square my homely lattice overlooks.

VALORI.

May I not go with you?

CANDIDA.

                    No, stay and act.
Defend the Commonwealth; and that will be
Petition and thanksgiving all at once.
Now, now, I pray, release me; for the eyes
Of those that love not, delicacy lack
To judge of them that do.

VALORI.

                    When shall we meet?

CANDIDA.

Why, always!   All my days are henceforth yours.
Yours will be mine, when nobly occupied.
            [They separate.   Exit CANDIDA (right).]

VALORI.

O, I am sated with my happiness!
Gods! send me a woe a little, that I may
Recover my lost appetite for joy!
            [VALORI turns to leave (left).   As he does so, LUCA
                CORSINI, DOMENICO BONSI, and GUIDANTONIO
                VESPUCCI enter (left).]

SCENE V.

VALORI.

I greet you, gentlemen!

[Exit.]

CORSINI.

His glance is bright.
But often so are suns before they set.
I ween his day is over.

BONSI.

It may be
The austere Candida has smiled on him.
Reasons of State could lend him no such glow.

VESPUCCI.

I saw a troop of gallants yesterday,
Who wagered his destruction: cousins all
Of Tornabuoni he denounced to death.

CORSINI.

Ha! have they then returned?   Significant!
When storks fly back to roofs that have been fired,
It shows the flames are out that ravaged them!

BONSI

Perhaps not out, but turned the other way,
'Gainst those that flashed the flint.

VESPUCCI.

It is the hour
Denoted for the Ordeal of Fire.
We ought to have been there.

CORSINI.

Too childish work !
Fit for the fools that gape at *tombola!*
Yet licensed by the Signory !

BONSI.

'Chance more wise
In that indulgence than in many a stroke
Reputed statecraft.   Here is one that comes,
Likely can tell us how 'tis prospering.

[Enter SODERINI (right).]

Say, come you from the Ordeal ?

SODERINI.

Straight and swift.

VESPUCCI.

Who has been burnt?

CORSINI.

Why, surely all of them.

SODERINI.

Nay, not a cowl nor single sandal scorched.
A splendid fire! an appetising fire!
But not a single friar to be fried.

BONSI.

Came they not then?

SODERINI.

O yes, they came in shoals,
Franciscans and Dominicans alike,
And went away again. 'Twas holy sport.

[Enter CEI (right).]

Was it not, Cei? Tell these gentlemen.

CEI.

'Tis easy told. The Loggia de' Lanzi
Was split in half: half to Saint Dominick,

And t' other to Saint Francis.　I should count
At least two hundred champions from Saint Mark's,
Headed by Frà Domenico; with these,
Marcuccio Salviati and his train,
Who with his sword a line upon the ground
Irately scratched, vowing that he who crossed
Should taste his point.

VESPUCCI.

But Spini sure was there?

SODERINI.

Briskly he was, and round him all his lads,
Spangled with arms, and phalanxed underneath
The Tetto de' Pisani.　'Twixt the twain,
Stood soldiers of the Signory and filled
All the Piazza, save the platformed space
That, hedged with fagots, pine-cones, resin, oil,
Stretched out for forty braccia.

CEI.

And behind
Packed close as Lenten herrings, fifties deep,
Peered all the eyes that love a miracle;

And every roof and window in the Square
Was cloyed with folk like branches when bees swarm.

CORSINI.

But where was Savonarola?

SODERINI.

　　　　　　　He was there,
Raimented white and carrying the Host,
Close by the side of Frà Domenico;
He habited in crimson, and his hands
Clasping a massive crucifix.　In truth,
Flickered no fear on either countenance,
But that fixed glow my mother says is Faith,
And which, I own, I never yet have seen
Saving upon men's faces when they pray.

BONSI.

And where were the Franciscans?

CEI.

　　　　　　　In the Square,
In their half of the Loggia; but appeared
Neither their champion Frà Giuliano, nor
The Frà Francesco that abetted him.

They with the Signory were closeted,
Too worldly wise to try if fire will burn,
Yet pressingly bewildered how to shirk
The hollow challenge solidly received
By mystic rivals.

SODERINI.

Suddenly it was urged
That Frà Domenico's red velvet cope
Might be enchanted by the demon spells
Of Frà Girolamo.   Forthwith 'twas doffed.
What, Cei, plea came next? for I forget.

CEI.

'Twas laughable.   They made him change his vest
With one of the Franciscans.   Then they cried
He must remove from Frà Girolamo,
So that no hocus-pocus might be tried,
And stand 'mong the Franciscans.

BONSI.

To these tests
What answered Frà Domenico?

SODERINI.

Never blenched,

But fix'dly clasped his crucifix.   O, he played
The fanatic to perfection.   Only when
It was proposed to take that last poor help
Out of his hands, and send him on alone
Into the flames, he seemed to hesitate,
And prayed he might exchange it for the Host.
Then rose there such a hubbub as you hear
In o'erstocked rookeries at Whitsuntide
When the young birds are harried in their haunts.
A clatter of theology began :
Some shouted "sacrilege !" while some harangued
About "essential substance" "accidents,"
And suchlike fond conceits.   The Signory
Cut short their long scholastic, and announced
The Ordeal deferred.   See !   Here they come,
The disappointed rabble.

CORSINI.

Let us go.
The after-drip of folly damps as much
As doth the storm itself.

> [Exeunt CORSINI, BONSI, and VESPUCCI (left).   CEI
> and SODERINI remain.   A crowd, composed of
> PIAGNONI, COMPAGNACCI, and ARRABBIATI indis-
> criminately, comes on (right).]

T

FIRST ARRABBIATO.

A trap ! a sham !

A hollow business !

FIRST PIAGNONE.

Whose fault was that ?

SECOND ARRABBIATO.

Why, whose but your prophetic shavenpate's,
Whose prophesyings ever come to nought ?

SECOND PIAGNONE.

He did not prophesy the Ordeal.

FIRST COMPAGNACCIO.

But, when 'twas there, why did he shrink from it ?

SODERINI.

Answer that riddle ; if he wants to show
He is inspired, why not confront the flames
And make no more ado ?

CEI.

And not stand by
Arguing, while others proffer to be burnt.

SECOND COMPAGNACCIO.

And are not burnt, nor even so much as singed,
Though everything they stickled for was trim
As faith could wish.

THIRD PIAGNONE.

　　　　　　　Exactly what I feel.
A miracle was fairly due to us,
An actual downright patent miracle;
No visions, and stale juggleries of that sort,
But a good noonday miracle; one we could see,
And none could doubt about.

SECOND COMPAGNACCIO.

　　　　　　　Now, do you think,
Were he in league with Heaven, he'd hesitate
To stand in hissing turpentine all day,
Like to the saints of old?　What say you, man?

SECOND PIAGNONE.

I can say nothing; only that I wish
That Frà Girolamo had faced the Fire,
And made an end of it.

SECOND COMPAGNACCIO.

                    End of himself.
Leave him alone ; he knows what he's about.

FIRST ARRABBIATO.

Ay, that he does, the tonsured charlatan ;
A rank impostor.

SECOND PIAGNONE.

                    Nay, he is not that.

SECOND ARRABBIATO.

What is he, then ?   A prophet, I suppose ?

SECOND PIAGNONE.

I did not say he was.

FIRST COMPAGNACCIO.

                    If he is not,
What is the good of him ?

TAILOR.

                    Such swindling work,
To lure industrious folks from off their stools

With promise of a miracle, and then
Befool them with a wrangle !

COBBLER.

In the time
I wasted gaping there, I could have made
Two uppers and a last.   A sorry scene !
I've done with friars.

FIRST CITIZEN.

And so have I.

SECOND CITIZEN.

And I.

[Shouting is heard. The Crowd turn in the direction
whence it proceeds ; and SPINI, followed by a
band of armed COMPAGNACCI, rushes upon the
stage.]

SPINI.

A San Marco !   A San Marco col Fuoco !

COMPAGNACCI.

On, comrades, to St. Mark's !

CEI.

What does he mean ?

SODERINI.

You trust to him for that.

Whate'er he says, that echo !

> [SPINI waves his sword, and again cries, "To Saint
> Mark's !" The cry is taken up universally, and
> the air rings with the shout.]

ALL.

A San Marco col Fuoco !   A San Marco col Fuoco !

> [The Crowd follow SPINI off the stage.   The scene
> changes.]

SCENE VI.

THE PIAZZA OF SAN MARCO.

[The façade of the Church occupies the centre of the back of the
stage.   On either side of it is an archway, through which
the side-walls of the Church and the Convent of San Marco
can be seen.   On the right are houses.   The doors of the
Church are open, and people, mostly women, can be
seen kneeling and praying inside.   A girl rises from her
knees, crosses herself, turns, and walks towards the doorway.   It is CANDIDA.   As she reaches the atrium of the
Church, enter VALORI hurriedly (left).   CANDIDA descends
the steps.

VALORI.

Love, have you prayed ?

CANDIDA.

As ne'er I prayed before.
My heart was brimming over, and it felt
As if we prayed together.

VALORI.

So we did;
And never moment needed more our prayer.
All the air whispers danger.   You must go,
And keep within your house.   'Tis there, is't not?

CANDIDA.

Yes, with a garden of my own behind :
When will you see it?   I would show it you.
There is a belt of pinks, christened quite wrong,
For white, all white, and scented like the clove;
A running riband of perfumèd snow,
Which the hot sun is melting rapidly.
When will you come?

VALORI.

When I have peril pushed
A blade's length further off?

CANDIDA.

Is it so grave?

VALORI.

No, no, 'tis nothing.   I will see to it.
Go to your garden.

CANDIDA.

Then, behind the pinks,
Are ostentatious marigolds that flaunt
Their buxom wealth i' the sun; tall poppy stems
Almost as long as your sword, and O, with heads
Plump as a gourd; light-nodding meadow-sweet,
Gracious as plume of gallant cavalier
Throned on his steed; and modest mignonette,
That, nowhere seen, surmised is everywhere.

VALORI.

So unpretentious virtue sweetens life.
I long to see it.

CANDIDA.

Round my casement blow
Those clustering roses fancy hath baptized
Maids-of-the-Village; and adown they hang,
Like to a waterfall you see far off,
That foams but moves not.   O come soon, or they
Will all be shattered.

VALORI.

Life were too sweet, too sweet,
With these and thee ! I scarce can think that Heaven
Hath kept this Heaven upon the hither side
For my poor lump of earth, save heavenly thou
Exorcise my mortality !   But hark !

[Loud shouts are heard, hard-by.]

There ! go, my love ! and in your garden stay !

CANDIDA.

And wait there till you come ?   You will come soon ?
O, you should smell it when the first faint stars
Peep through the darkening lattice of the sky,
To see if night be coming : better still,
When 'tis in stealthy darkness muffled up,
And drenched with dew invisible.

VALORI.

To-night !
And when the times are sweeter, many a night
We'll savour it together.

[CANDIDA retires into her house.   VALORI passes under
　　the archway (right), and disappears round an angle
　　of the wall.   Shouts again are heard proceeding
　　from the back of the Convent.   There is a panic

in the Church, from which women and children rush and disappear in every direction. Inside the Church are now a number of Monks, some of them armed. Conspicuous among them is Bettuccio, now Frà Benedetto, wearing the habit of Dominick, but with a breastplate over it, and brandishing a sword. Simultaneously, a number of Arrabbiati pour into the Square, and attempt to enter the Church. The Monks resist, fighting with rude weapons, some of them with heavy church candlesticks and candelabra, one Monk laying about him with a massive metal crucifix. The assailants are beaten off. At this juncture Savonarola appears in the doorway of the Church, attended by Frà Domenico.]

SAVONAROLA.

Lay down your arms, my children.   'Tis through me

This tempest hath arisen, I must lay;

And with my blood it will assuagëd be.

Into their hands I will surrender me,

My enemies, to do what sooth they will.

FRÀ DOMENICO.

O Father! you must not abandon us!

They for your life are thirsting.   What shall we do,

If once you leave us?

SAVONAROLA.

      Then, my children, form

Yourselves into procession ; we will pass

Along the cloister, thence into the choir,

And there before the Eucharist will sing

Salvum fac populum tuum, Domine !

Frà Benedetto ! put away that sword,

And take the Cross.   No follower of mine

Must shed man's blood, unless it be his own

In stream of sacrifice !   Now, chant the hymn !

> [The Procession is formed, and they pass up the Church
> singing. The doors are closed and bolted. Shouts
> again are heard ; and another band of COMPA-
> GNACCI and ARRABBIATI enter (left), headed by
> SPINI.

SPINI.

Ha ! they are shut.   Then waste we not our blows

Battering their stubbornness.   This way, my lads !

I know a tenderer entrance.

> [They pass under the archway (left), and disappear. At
> the same moment VALORI lets himself down from
> the top of the Convent wall (right), and is followed
> by MARCUCCIO SALVIATI. They both come through
> the archway (right) on to the body of the stage.]

VALORI.

Go, then, quick,

And bring us at your heels what help you can ;

And I will hasten to the Signory,

And rouse their apathy.

> [Exit SALVIATI (right). VALORI turns to cross the stage and pass out (left). Enter (left) six Gentlemen armed.]

FIRST GENTLEMAN.

See! Here he is! Now then to finish him.

We are Lorenzo Tornabuoni's kin,

And his pretence survives upon our points.

Defend yourself!

> [VALORI draws, and for a moment he parries their attacks. A fresh Crowd surges into the square. CANDIDA comes out of her house (right), and rushes towards VALORI, who is run through the body at the same moment, while she receives a thrust that was meant for him. Both fall. The Crowd rush, shouting, under 'each archway (right and left), and the Kindred of TORNABUONI hurry off, the wounded forms of VALORI and CANDIDA alone occupying the stage.]

CANDIDA.

I wish that I had loved you, love, before.

VALORI.

I wish you had! But many things come late

In this unpunctual world!

CANDIDA.

Yet, love, it is
Only a separation.   We shall meet,
A little minute hence.

VALORI.

Art clear of that ?
For I have been so busy with the State
In these sad times, that I had utterly
Forgot my soul.

CANDIDA.

That's a forgetfulness
God will remember, and absolve you, dear.
Who loves his country never forfeits Heaven.

VALORI.

Have you strength left to kiss me, Candida ?
Even in Heaven touch of those lips would be
A blessëd recollection.   See !   I am here !

[He stretches out his hand, and by it she draws herself towards him.]

Is that your garden that I smell ?   How sweet !

> [They die ; her lips on his. Shouts again are heard ;
> and COMPAGNACCI and ARRABBIATI pour through
> both archways into the Square. SODERINI, who
> is amongst them, notices the dead bodies, and
> throws his cloak over them.]

SODERINI.

Wedded, at last.   O enviable pair !

SPINI.

These shavelings make the stubbornest defence
That ever I encountered.   We must go
And roll up more attack.

CEI.

                    Ay, that we must.
Scores of our chaps lie sprawling at the foot
Of the Convent Wall.

SPINI.

                    Then let us lose no time.
Look you ! the sun is down.

> [They disappear, and the body of the stage is unoccupied.
> At that moment, the doors of the Church are
> thrown open. SAVONAROLA appears, carrying the
> Host, and surrounded by his Brethren.]

SAVONAROLA.

This your defence I bid you cease, and here,

Here before God, my sons, before His Host,
With enemies around you swarming, I
Confirm to you my doctrine.   What I taught,
From God I had, and that I lie not, He
My witness is in Heaven !   I did not think
Against me would so swift this city turn.
But now God's will be done!   My last request,
My final exhortation, is but this :
Faith, patience, prayer, your only weapons be !
With anguish do I quit you all, to go
Into my enemies' hands.   I cannot say
If they will take my life; but this is sure,
That, dead, I can in Heaven assist you more,
Than ever here on earth.   Be comforted.
Hold fast the Cross, and with it you will find
The portals of Salvation!

> [Shouts again are heard, and the COMPAGNACCI, ARRAB-
> BIATI, and Populace, return to the Piazza.   With
> them are armed Officers of the SIGNORY. SAVONA-
> ROLA stands mute, with the Host in his hand,
> surrounded by his brethren, FRÀ DOMENICO and
> FRÀ SILVESTRO being on either side of him.]

OFFICER OF THE SIGNORY.

I am here
With orders from the Signory to claim

And lead away as prisoners of State,
Savonarola, Frà Domenico,
And Frà Silvestro.

SAVONAROLA.

Here we stand, unarmed.

[He hands the Host to one of the Monks, and advances.
Then he turns to the Brethren.]

SAVONAROLA.

Mind you, my children, never must you doubt
The work of the Lord will still march on apace.
My death will only hasten it.

[SAVONAROLA offers himself a prisoner to the Officers,
and FRÀ DOMENICO and FRÀ SILVESTRO do the
same. They are bound with cords and led down
the steps. The Crowd shout, surround SAVONA-
ROLA, mock and insult him, as he is led away.
The Curtain falls.]

END OF ACT IV.

ACT V.

SCENE I.

A Street in Florence.

[At the right of the stage, a small open Loggia, raised
above the level of the stage by three steps, and
up which clamber Banksia roses in full bloom.
Inside the Loggia are seated Corsini, Bonsi, and
Vespucci. On the left of the stage, facing them,
are the northern parts of the city, Fiesole, Careggi,
· Monte Morello, and the spurs of the Apennines.]

CORSINI.

How passing fair the city looks to-day.

BONSI.

Yes, and how fresh her territory, robed
In the abundant greenery of May !
Quick-scaling roses have surprised the walls,
And the Valdarno laughs beneath the spears
Of serried growth in peaceful phalanx ranged.
Methinks I scent the clover even here.

U

VESPUCCI.

Likely enough; and note you how afar,
Melted by winsomeness of childlike Spring,
The manly mountains wear a feminine smile.
Scarcely a day for such a sight as that
Hourly preparing.

CORSINI.

   Are all three to die?
'Twas said the Bishop of Ilerda strove
To rescue Frà Domenico.

BONSI.

    If he did,
'Twas feebly argued. Answered, he not dead,
Savonarola's doctrine would survive,
Curtly the Pope's Commissioner replied,
" One friar more or less—what matters it?
Then burn him too."

VESPUCCI.

    . He seems the stubborn sort.
Torture, they say, but tightened constancy ;
And when they vouched him Frà Girolamo
Himself himself forswore, he sat him down,

And wrote unto the brethren of Saint Mark,
Enjoining them to bind up all the works
Of Frà Girolamo, nor fail to keep
One copy in the library, and one
In the refectory, securing them
Unto the lectern by a little chain.

CORSINI.

Think you that Savonarola did confess
His prophecies imposture?

BONSI.

　　　　　　　　Possibly.
The visionary's valour, that is fledged
In watches of uncontradicting night
Or sympathising solitude, and wings
Limitless flight through unresisting space,
Confronted by the sharp and alien air
Of earthly circumstance,—well, droops and flags.

VESPUCCI.

Doubtless, you probe it there.　Vigil and fast,
Obeisant brethren, and the duping shout
Of crowds that foster frenzy, rarefied

His mind to vapour; which was back condensed
By the chill silence of a prison cell,
The face of cold inquisitors, the tramp
Of deaf, dumb gaolers, all the accidents
That render doubt substantial.

CORSINI.

Nor forget
The grimly real rack with grinning teeth,
The sceptic cords, the idealising brain
Helpless to serve the body in that pinch,
And Heaven not intervening!

BONSI.

Yet they say,
When last upon the rack stretched out afresh,
That he recanted every utterance
Discrediting his prophecies, and prayed
God would condone the frailty of the flesh
Which had denied Him, and that now he stands
Fast by that gospel.   Here comes one that was
The worldly arm of the Frateschi till
Themselves had learned more worldliness.

[Enter SALVIATI (right), with his eyes upon the ground.]

VESPUCCI.

How now,

Good Salviati?

SALVIATI.

I am good no more,
Save to be exiled, if that suits my foes:
An officer whose privates have dispersed,
A flag without a following.

CORSINI.

How is that?

SALVIATI.

Why, even I, dull though I am, could see
On what a narrow and ambiguous edge
Florence was treading.　I am a soldier, sirs:
Enjoy no visions, ask no miracles,
Under my breastplate no raw hair-shirt hide,
But served the State, while still Valori lived,
With some fidelity.　But those daft loons
I pressed into my service had conceived
Praying would starve out Pisa, hymns persuade
The plague to pass elsewhere, and wealth increase

By burning of their luxuries.   When they found
Cause was not crowned with consequence,—well, they
The Cause abandoned.

BONSI.

                    Have they all forsworn
The prophesying Prior?

SALVIATI.

                    Nearly all:
All saving credulous women.   They stand firm,
Believing more, the more a thing's disproved.
Withal, Heaven bless them!   They are like the dew
That comes with morning and returns with night,
And having cheered some luminary's dawn,
Shrink back into themselves when he rides high,
That they may soothe his setting.   With your leave,
I will continue homewards, for I am
A trifle sad.

                              [Exit SALVIATI (right).]

VESPUCCI.

                    That's a straightforward man,
Entangled in the ravel of these times.
But he will cut it, for he has a sword.

These men of action tread the easiest road.
'Tis only thought's inextricable mesh
Makes life confusion.

BONSI.

                    Cease we then to think !
How softly doth the landscape kiss the eyes !
Let us awhile look on it quietly.

VESPUCCI.

There will not be much quietness to-day.
Look !   Here they come.

SCENE II.

THE SAME.

[A number of Citizens enter (left). FRATESCHI, ARRABBIATI,
    and PIAGNONI ; but the FRATESCHI and PIAGNONI have
    discarded their distinctive garb.]

CORSINI.

                    Let us listen to their talk,
'Twill edify good sense.

FIRST ARRABBIATO.

So you're convinced

He's an impostor ?

FIRST PIAGNONE.

Who can doubt of it ?
Why, hasn't he confessed it with his hand ?

SECOND ARRABBIATO.

And you, my comrade ?

SECOND PIAGNONE.

Thoroughly satisfied.
Here is the copy of a letter sent
By friars of San Marco to the Pope.
Want you to hear ?

FIRST PIAGNONE.

Yes, read it ; and speak up.

SECOND PIAGNONE.

[Reads aloud.]

" Not only we, but men of much greater penetra-
tion, were taken in by the astuteness of Frà Girolamo.
The correctness of his doctrine, the rectitude of his

life, the sanctity of his manners, his ostensible devotion, the reputation he acquired by expelling from the city evil customs, usury, and every feature of vice, the many events which, foretold and verified beyond the power of mere human imagination, confirmed his prophecies;—all these were so striking, that if he himself had not recanted, avowing that his words did not proceed from God, we never should have been able to withdraw our faith from him.   And so thoroughly did we believe in him, that we were all ready to expose our bodies at the stake in confirmation of his doctrine. Let it satisfy your Holiness to have got hold of the source and origin of our errors, Frà Girolamo Savonarola.   Let him bear the fitting penalty, if such can be devised, for so much wickedness.   We, poor strayed sheep, return to the true shepherd."

THIRD PIAGNONE.

What more can any one want ?   Proof positive
This Prior was a charlatan.

FOURTH PIAGNONE.

A rogue.

'Tis patent as a syllogism.

CORSINI.

                    But, friends !
How if this recantation spurious be ?

[BETTUCCIO, who has entered (right), comes forward,
        with a paper in his hand.]

BETTUCCIO.

As specious, spurious, lying, sure it is.

FIRST ARRABBIATO.

Bettuccio !

SECOND ARRABBIATO.

            Nay, Frà Benedetto now,
Gone cracked since they interred his lady-love !

BETTUCCIO.

Where is the autograph Process ?   'Tis destroyed.
Where the four hundred ducats, promised bribe
To Ser Ceccone, the false notary ?
He gets but fifty ; for his dirty work
Has proved not foul enough.   And tell me this :
Why were two hundred citizens shut out
From the Grand Council when the Signory
Elected was anew ?   Why Doffo Spini,
His first, his worst, his bitterest enemy,

Placed on the jury that examined him ?
Why never in his presence, nor before
All the Grand Council, was the Process read,
As is by law appointed ?

FIRST PIAGNONE.
Why, because
Savonarola feared he would be stoned.

BETTUCCIO.

Afraid of being stoned ! Then go and see
This coward die. But ere you go, hear this.
This is a later Process, garbled too,
But with the truth not utterly shut out.

VOICES.

Enough of Processes !

OTHER VOICES.
More than enough !
[A number of people, running, enter (left).]

FIRST CITIZEN.

Come on, good folks ! Come quick ! Or you'll be
    late.

FIRST ARRABBIATO.

What !   Is it time ?

SECOND PIAGNONE.

Then let us go !

ALL.

Come on !

[Exeunt all (right), save CORSINI, BONSI, and BETTUCCIO.]

BONSI.

[To BETTUCCIO.]

You might as well distinguish with the wind,
As intercept the crowd's conclusion
By pointing to the premiss.   When this storm
Is beggared of its fury, write a book,
And tell the world of this strange episode.
You poets are the best historians,
And in your cloister, novice, you will have
Abundant leisure.

[To CORSINI and VESPUCCIO.]

Shall we go in to breakfast ?

[The Scene changes.]

SCENE III.

PIAZZA OF THE SIGNORIA.

[Three Tribunals or Galleries, with their back to the Palazzo
    Pubblico. In one is the Bishop of VASONA, in his Epis-
    copal robes; in the second, the Papal Commissioners,
    GIOACCHINO TURRIANO, General of the Dominicans, and
    FRANCESCO ROMOLINO, Bishop of Ilerda; in the third,
    the SIGNORY. From these to the middle of the Piazza
    runs an elevated wooden way, at the end of which rises a
    tall strong stake, with a cross-beam near the top of it.
    From this cross-beam hang three halters and three chains.
    Round the stake is a heap of inflammable material. Foot-
    soldiers of the SIGNORY prevent the people from approach-
    ing it. The Piazza is crowded with persons of all ranks,
    ages, and conditions.]

FIRST CITIZEN.

How like a cross that looks.

SECOND CITIZEN.

                        And looked more like,
Until the Signory, perceiving it,
Sawed off the top.

THIRD CITIZEN.

                    It still looks like a cross.

A WOMAN.

It looks like what it is.

FIRST ARRABBIATO.

                    I almost think
They might have spared his life.   It had sufficed
To lodge him in close durance.

SECOND ARRABBIATO.

                              For how long?
For aught we know, another Signory
Had set him free, and then we should have had
This pother o'er again.

THIRD ARRABBIATO.

                    Best as it is.
An enemy that's dead makes war no more.

FIRST PIAGNONE.

Why, even now, men scatter through the streets
His Commentary on the Psalms, "*In Te
Domine, speravi*," writ by him in prison.

SECOND PIAGNONE.

And a long Meditation late conceived,

Upon the *Miserere ;* and 'tis said
He has again been prophesying ill
That is to fall on Florence when there reigns
A Pope called Clement.

FIRST ARRABBIATO.

　　　　　　　Borgia had the wit
To avoid that name, which would have lent a foil
Too glaring 'gainst his nature.　Are not those
The Pope's Commissioners ?

SECOND ARRABBIATO.

　　　　　　　Hush !　Here they come.

[Enter SAVONAROLA, FRÀ DOMENICO, and FRÀ SIL-
VESTRO, barefoot.　A Crier steps forward.]

CRIER.

The Gonfaloniere and the Eight,
Having the Processes considered well
Of the three Friars, and the grievous crimes
Therein contained, and having, most of all,
Considered the Pope's sentence, which condemns
And so consigns them to the secular arm,
That they be punished, hereby do pronounce :
That each of these three Friars do first be hanged,

Then burnt, until their souls be utterly
Dissevered from their bodies.

> [SAVONAROLA and his companions are led forward to
> the front of the Tribunal where the BISHOP OF
> VASONA sits, and are stripped of their outer habit,
> and left standing in long linen tunics.]

SAVONAROLA.

O sacred habit! how I cherished thee !
Thou unto me wast given by grace of God,
And spotless have I kept thee to the end.
Now do I not relinquish thee, but thou
Art taken from me !

FRÀ SILVESTRO.

      Into Thy hands, O Lord,
I commend my spirit.

FRÀ DOMENICO.

      Bear this well in mind,
The prophecies of Frà Girolamo
Will all be verified.   For us, we die
Innocent.

> [The BISHOP, who has descended from the Tribunal,
> takes hold of the arm of SAVONAROLA.]

BISHOP.

I separate thee from the Church
Militant and triumphant !

SAVONAROLA.

There, you trip !
Militant, yes !   Triumphant ?   'Tis not yours !

[He turns and walks along the platform to the place of
     execution, with FRÀ DOMENICO on his right, and
     FRÀ SILVESTRO on the left.   CEI and SODERINI
     emerge from the crowd.]

CEI.

Nay, come away!   'Twill be a loathsome sight.
There is a plaguing voice within my heart,
Whispers me we were wrong to plug our ears
Against the heavenly thunders of this Friar.

SODERINI.

A melancholy end !

CEI.

What end is not ?
Yet different means breed different ends, be sure.

X

His name will live while life and death endure ;

But as for these, his executioners,

Their very memory with their bones will rot,

And only slimy worms remember them !

[The Curtain falls.]

THE END.

Printed by R. & R. CLARK, *Edinburgh*.